Bolan heard a thunk on the trail beside him

Whirling, he raked the shadows with the M-16, searching for a target. He found nothing. And then he saw it—a severed head near his feet.

Suddenly a tall form slid out of the woods to face Bolan. Lightning bathed the dark figure of Lev Belokai. Bolan watched the death's head grin on the assassin's face, blood still dripping from the Russian's Kukri knife.

"Executioner," the KGB killer said. "I know who you are, but this is not the time for us yet. We shall meet again, in a very cold place." He motioned toward the trail with the blade. "Like him, your head next."

Bolan raised the M-16 to end it. But at that moment the lightning strobed again, and when the gloom cloaked the forest moments later, there was no sign of Belokai. Not even a shadow. Only the wind, the rain and the darkness.

MACK BOLAN

The Executioner

DON PENDLETON's EXECUTIONER

MACK BOLAN

Black Dice

A GOLD EAGLE BOOK FROM

W☉RLDWIDE

TORONTO • NEW YORK • LONDON • PARIS
AMSTERDAM • STOCKHOLM • HAMBURG
ATHENS • MILAN • TOKYO • SYDNEY

First edition February 1987

ISBN 0-373-61098-X

Special thanks and acknowledgment to
Dan Schmidt for his contributions to this work.

Printed in Canada

Nothing can excuse a general who takes advantage of the knowledge acquired in the service of his country, to deliver up her frontier and her towns to foreigners. This is a crime reprobated by every principle of religion, morality and honor.

—Napoleon, *Maxims of War*, 1831

Treason is tantamount to murder, and the traitor must be prepared to forfeit his or her life.

—Mack Bolan

THE
MACK BOLAN
LEGEND

Nothing less than a war could have fashioned the destiny of the man called Mack Bolan. Bolan earned the Executioner title in the jungle hellgrounds of Vietnam, for his skills as a crack sniper in pursuit of the enemy.

But this supreme soldier also wore another name—Sergeant Mercy. He was so tagged because of the compassion he showed to wounded comrades-in-arms and Vietnamese civilians.

Mack Bolan's second tour of duty ended prematurely when he was given emergency leave to return home and bury his family. Bolan made his peace at his parents' and sister's gravesite. Then he declared war on the evil force that had snatched his loved ones. The Mafia.

In a fiery one-man assault, he confronted the Mob head-on, carrying a cleansing flame to the urban menace. And when the battle smoke cleared, a solitary figure walked away alive.

He continued his lone-wolf struggle, and soon a hope of victory began to appear. But Mack Bolan had broken society's every rule. That same society started gunning for this elusive warrior—to no avail.

So Bolan was offered amnesty to work within the system against international terrorism. This time, as an official employee of Uncle Sam, Bolan wore yet another handle: Colonel John Phoenix. With government sanction now, and a command center at Stony Man Farm in Virginia's Blue Ridge Mountains, he and his new allies—Able Team and Phoenix Force—waged relentless war on a new adversary: the KGB and all it stood for.

Until the inevitable occurred. Bolan's one true love, the brilliant and beautiful April Rose, died at the hands of the Soviet terror machine.

Embittered and utterly saddened by this feral deed, Bolan broke the shackles of Establishment authority.

Now the big justice fighter is once more free to haunt the treacherous alleys of the shadow world.

1

The night belonged to Death.

And the big man wearing combat black belonged to the night.

Yeah, death was in the air, Mack Bolan decided. He didn't have to see it in the flesh to know its ugly presence. It was something he lived with constantly. Death was a force the man known as the Executioner now felt, beckoning him into the maw of the Allegheny Mountain forest.

Thunder cannoned across the coal-black sky and lightning stroked the darkness. Bolan's ice-blue eyes glinted for a second against the violent electrical flash. From the rumbling heavens rain pelted the foliage around the lone stalker, masking his penetration of the perimeter of the CIA safehouse.

With the silenced Beretta 93-R in hand, the Man from Blood ghosted swiftly through the shadows. As more lightning crackled overhead, something on the trail ahead caught Bolan's eye. He stopped, crouched. What he discovered he didn't dare touch, or step in. The giant bear trap would have snapped his leg in half.

Okay, he thought, so they were damned serious about protecting their ComBloc boy. Hard-line intel from Hal Brognola back in D.C. had already made that clear. Now the big nightfighter suspected he was up against something that could turn this rainy night into a quagmire of blood. Brognola's words still sent a shiver down Bolan's spine. And knotted his guts with a cold rage.

Defectors. Spies. Both American and Soviet. It was something that had been going on for years, Bolan knew. Hell, since the beginning of time, when men, nations, became a threat to each other. But until Brognola's briefing Bolan hadn't been aware of the extent, the depth of treachery by his own countrymen, right under his nose. Bolan wanted Army intelligence officers Ron Snipes and John Dover. Bad.

For the past ten years, according to Brognola, those bastards had been selling vital secrets about American weapons systems to the Soviets. No telling what the traitors had been selling lately. Brognola suspected that vital info about the Strategic Defense Initiative was being leaked to the Russians by Uncle Sam's money-hungry vultures. Star Wars, the press called it. SDI. Any way Bolan sliced it, it was treason. A traitor was just a slightly different breed of cannibal.

Mack Bolan carried the medicine for that particular disease.

But he needed leverage to get to Snipes and Dover.

Fifty yards ahead, Bolan saw the CIA safehouse where Company operatives were holding Andrey Baknov. He was a Soviet defector, who claimed to have a master list of planned KGB terrorist activities around the world.

Bolan wanted Baknov. And that master list. And the two American vultures.

First things first, though. The CIA wanted Baknov as leverage to get the traitors back, too. And if the CIA wanted to hold the deck, then Mack Bolan intended to be the wild card that spoiled everybody's hand.

As Bolan closed in on the log cabin he found that he had company. That company toted an assault rifle. Bad company.

Bolan holstered the Beretta in the speed rig beneath his left arm. He opted to go with his garrote, a tongue loosener. Big Thunder, the stainless-steel .44 AutoMag hand cannon, hung in quick-draw leather strapped to his right hip. The heavy firepower. The firepower he would unleash when the tongues had been loosened and were ready to be ripped out.

Crouched, Bolan scoured the woods in every direction. He searched the forest floor through the lightning flashes for any shadows, for any other invaders. He saw none.

Bolan closed in on the lone invader. The guy began to turn toward Bolan, his eyes widening with surprise and fear. Bolan looped the wire around the invader's neck, cutting off the man's cry of alarm. That face of fear beneath him turned into a mask of shock and horror. The Executioner twisted the garrote, the wire biting into flesh, drawing a line of crimson across the scrawny neck in his grasp. The M-16 dropped into the brush as Bolan's hand grabbed at the garrote.

"That's just to let you know I'm serious, guy," Bolan breathed. "Dead serious. I'm not going to kill you. Unless you want it."

Thunder boomed. Lightning flashed. The Executioner's prey struggled for a moment, then went limp with terror.

"Who...are y-you?" the bearded, long-haired prey croaked, gasping for air. "Wh-what—"

"I'll ask the questions. For starters you tell me who you are and what you're doing here."

Long-hair hesitated, but the Executioner tightened his hold.

"L-listen, man, I dunno who the hell you think you are, but you're making a big mistake."

"I'll be the judge of that. You've got one second to start spouting...or start praying."

"Okay, okay," Long-hair blurted, fingers clawing at the wire. "We want that Russian bastard in there. What's it to you?"

"Who's we?"

"The Long Knives, man. Fucking Snake Eyes. He sent us out here to see if we could snatch the Russki. Snake Eyes, he's the leader, man. Said we don't pass this initiation we're out of the group. We're patriots, and having this Russki right under our noses don't sit well with Snake."

Patriots, Bolan thought wryly. More like vigilante fanatics who would just as soon gun down a CIA agent as they would a Russian, in service of their twisted cause. As far as Bolan was concerned, the Long Knives were just a pack of riffraff. A lynch mob. A hate group. The scum in his grasp now looked, smelled and talked like nothing more than an outlaw biker. Spell that one-percenter. Loser.

"Keep talking," Bolan demanded. "I haven't heard enough to let you keep breathing."

"Hey, man, I-I'm havin' a tough time talkin' if I can't even breathe."

"You'll be breathing through a slit in your throat in a second."

The Long Knife got the message, muttered a curse. "Milt . . . Freeman, that's Snake, said we're going to execute the Russian for the whole country to see. Show the world that patriots won't sit by and let these traitors play their game."

"How did Freeman know about this safehouse?"

"You stupid or what? How do you think? We've been watching the cabin for weeks. We know the score. CIA. KGB. It don't make no difference to the Long Knives. We want something bad enough, we take it. And we're taking back this country from all the shitheads trying to destroy it. The Jews. The niggers. The bleeding hearts."

Bolan was just about to ask the Long Knife if there were any other patriots in the forest when he spotted six shadows creeping up beside the cabin. He watched the shadows for a second, before they vanished behind the safehouse.

"Your buddies?" Bolan growled.

"Your death knell, boy," the Long Knife growled, feeling brave again. "The Long Knives are coming to take."

"You get back to this Freeman," Bolan warned. "Tell him to butt the hell out of this. You people cross me up again you'll have a war on your hands."

The Long Knife started to sputter a curse. But Bolan dropped Long-hair with a cracking right uppercut to the jaw. Silently, the Executioner wished this patriot a sleep full of stars, stripes and bleeding hearts.

Suddenly autofire erupted from the cabin ahead. Screams, rifle chatter, revolver blasts ripped through the storm-lashed night.

Death and dying had descended with the storm, the Executioner knew, the rain suddenly ice cold as it hammered his face, skull and neck.

Scooping up the Long Knife's M-16, Bolan set the assault rifle on full-auto, chambered a round.

The storm seemed to take on a sudden, relentless fury. Lightning flashed and thunder cannoned continuously, as if the sky had parted and given way to the wrath of the universe. Someone was about to feel the scourge of the universe. The Executioner hoped fate was on his side once again.

White flickering light silhouetted the warrior in black as he ran across the open ground, charging toward the cabin door.

Automatic weapon fire blistered on from inside the cabin. There was little doubt in the Executioner's mind as to who was winning the firefight. Cannibals had boiled up out of the night, and the CIA was getting its tail chewed.

Bolan stopped in front of the door, combat senses on full alert as adrenaline exploded through his blood. With Big Thunder filling his right fist, the seized M-16 in the other hand, Bolan caved in the cabin door with a kick that thundered in sync with nature's rage. The Executioner took the carnage in at a heartbeat. And was allowed even less time to react to high-voltage danger.

More autofire erupted from along the far wall, muzzle-flashes winking behind a thin curtain of orange kerosene light. Bolan moved like the lightning outside, spinning out of the doorway as 5.56 mm tumblers ravaged the wood beside his head. Zeroing in on the Long Knife shadows, Bolan triggered the M-16 and Big Thunder at once. The cabin seemed to rock with the Executioner's onslaught. Flesh-shredding .44 slugs, married with cut-down 7.62 mm NATO rifle cartridge casings, pounded the Long Knives back into the wall.

Bolan's M-16 stitched the dancing puppets as they jerked, twisted, crashed and caromed off one another. Bloody cloudbursts sprayed the wall, splashed the small radio console near the back doorway as 240-grain slugs, muzzling at 1640 feet per second, drilled through flesh and bone. A combined M-16–AutoMag roar launched a Long Knife through a double window. Wind and rain instantly washed over the fallen dead, the human sack flipping over the windowsill, vanishing.

For a long moment, the Executioner looked at the slaughterbed, his back braced against the wall. Arms, legs twitched around broken glass and wood splinters. Two kerosene lanterns swayed from the ceiling. Cold wind gusted, howled through the cabin.

Quickly, Bolan checked the dead men. Four CIA agents. Clean-cut. Cover-dressed in hunters' camous. No ID. Four Walther PPK/S handguns. Four HK-91 assault rifles. Not exactly the kind of hardware a deer hunter would be packing. No, Bolan figured, these guys had come prepared for war. But they'd lost the opening round to a pack of vigilante lunatics. And each of those six scruffy, denim- or leather-jacketed Long Knives inside and outside the cabin was now just bullet-churned trash. Casualties of their own fanaticism.

A groan sounded from near the far wall. Bolan whirled, spotted the agent as the man clambered into a sitting position against the wall.

Bolan moved, stood over the badly wounded agent.

Blood flecked the operative's lips. He stared at Bolan through glazed eyes, his hands folded over the bloody shreds of his stomach.

Bolan crouched, checked the guy's pulse. Weak. Gutshot and dying fast.

"These assholes weren't KGB," the agent sputtered. "Son of a...caught us by complete surprise. We thought we had secured...the area...."

Yeah, Bolan thought, the wild cards were gathering with the predators. It was getting damned near impossible to distinguish one from the other. Long Knives. KGB. And the spy chum that had drawn in all of the sharks. But Bolan found no Soviet defector among the dead.

"What's your name?" Bolan quietly asked, wanting to take the agent's mind off his pain, attempting to soften the operative up for some hard questioning.

"M-Marchetti," the Company man replied. "Mike. Special Operations Division."

Bolan didn't think an introduction on his part would help his cause. During his KGB wars, the CIA had put out a liquidation mandate on his head. He had been a dead man running. Back then, Bolan had been Colonel John Phoenix, the lone warrior who'd nearly crushed the Mafia monster single-handedly. The one-man crusader, scorching the vile, soulless monsters of organized crime, who'd been asked by Uncle Sam to come in from the cold and use his martial skills to take the fire and the sword to the terrorist butchers of the world.

The Company hadn't thought too much of Bolan-Phoenix's government-sanctioned war against terrorism. Particularly when agents were getting swept up in the cross fire hurricane, even though they weren't being cut down by the Bolan guns. The final days with

Stony Man Farm, Bolan's war base in the Blue Ridge Mountains of Virginia, had been a time of treachery, double-dealing and setups. A KGB mole, planted in the White House, had been responsible for the horror that had torn the warrior's life apart on a cold, stormy night, much like this one. A night when his greatest love, April Rose, had been butchered by the guns of treachery.

Those Stony Man days were as dead as April Rose. Mack Bolan was on his own again. The lone wolf in search of rabid meat. The way it was, should and would be until the day death snatched him.

Marchetti appeared to search Bolan's face for several moments, as if combing through his memory, trying to match the phantom face with a name.

"Marchetti," Bolan said, "where's Baknov?"

"Look, I don't know who the hell you are. W-why...should I tell you anything?"

"Because I may be able to save some lives. Starting with yours. If I can get some answers. The KGB has sent a murder squad for Baknov, right?"

Marchetti coughed up blood. Feebly, he nodded.

The agent seemed reluctant to tell Bolan anything more. But the Executioner waited.

"L-listen, mister," Marchetti said, "you aren't a Fed. And you're not from the Company. You want to help...you want my help, I want to know who I'm dealing with first. Understand?"

Bolan looked at the CIA man. He understood, all right. The cold war between the U.S. and Russia was getting set to turn hot. And the key answers to some of Bolan's questions were just a breath away from joining the night.

THE TALL, BROAD-SHOULDERED MAN with the bullet-shaped head seemed to materialize out of the flash of lightning. He moved with the swiftness and stealth of a predator. Rain slicked his black leather trench coat like a doughnut glaze. Lightning flashes, jagging through the forest, were mirrored by his slate-gray eyes, which seemed as cold and lifeless as a winter sky. As cold and empty as a tomb.

And Lev Belokai had come to turn the CIA safe-house into a CIA tomb.

Nyet, the KGB would suffer no failure in this matter, he decided.

The KGB's invisible Thirteenth Section had sent him to ensure victory over the CIA gangsters. The Committee for State Security had sent their elite killing machine, their master assassin. And Lev Belokai thought of himself as the *chistka*—the purge.

Belokai did not want to leave this night with no blood on his hands.

From the forest depths, he had seen the tall shadow take the fool with the long hair from behind. He had seen the shadow crush down the door to the safe-house, had heard the firefight. There was no doubt in Belokai's mind who had been the victor in that battle, and who that shadow was. But he wanted a closer look. A man did not climb the ranks of the Komitet

Gosudarstvennoi Bezopasnoati by acting on wild impulse. A true killer learned patience, thought through his every move before executing any single one of those moves.

Belokai angled toward the trail. As the fool stirred to life, the KGB assassin reached inside his trench coat, wrapped a leather-gloved fist around his Makarov pistol. The long-haired one would be no problem, Belokai decided. Still, he wanted the fool's blood. Belokai and his killteam had not penetrated the imperialist warmongering nation of degenerates only to be denied the blood of American pigs, nor, just as important, to be denied the head of the motherland's great traitor, Baknov, by the CIA.

Belokai would be denied nothing.

The KGB had come to take it all.

Belokai watched as the man lumbered to his feet, then bolted down the trail. Quickly, Belokai cut through the forest like a black phantom.

The assassin stepped out onto the trail.

The Long Knife turned, looked back. An expression of fear masking his features beneath the wet, matted tangles of hair, the Long Knife froze.

Slowly, Belokai stepped toward the Long Knife. "Do not move, American," the killer warned, raising the Makarov.

Lightning ripped, and the flash illuminated the bear trap, several feet behind the Long Knife.

Belokai saw the bear trap. The Long Knife didn't, as he stumbled in terror, backpedaling.

He stepped on the pan, released the spring. Razor-sharp metal teeth knifed into his leg, snapped bone. Twisting, his face contorted in agony, he toppled to the ground.

Belokai slapped a gloved palm over the wounded man's mouth, trapped part of the scream in his throat. With his weight, Belokai drove the Long Knife into the dirt.

A bloodied leg, jagged bone gleaming over the steel jaws, twitched behind Belokai. The KGB assassin felt a jolt of excitement, an electric tingle, as his captive convulsed beneath his grasp.

The Russian holstered his Makarov. From a leather sheath on his left hip, he slid a ceremonial Kukri knife free of its scabbard. A cold grin stretched Belokai's lips. The buffalo horn handle fitted his hand perfectly. Just as killing should be perfect, he thought, done by only the perfect assassin. The Gurkha soldier he'd slain in Nepal, the victim responsible for his possession of the Kukri, had been a perfect kill.

Belokai raised the Kukri above his head, savored the look of agony and horror he read in the fool's eyes.

"Do svidaniya," Belokai said, bidding the Long Knife goodbye.

Then the thick blade descended, chopping through the Long Knife's throat.

AT THE SOUND OF THE SCREAM, Bolan snapped hard-eyed attention toward the doorway. That scream had been a sound of mindless agony, choked off by something.

Or someone.

The Executioner holstered the AutoMag and moved across the cabin. He stopped beside the doorjamb, peered out into the night. Wind and rain whipped at his face as he stepped outside and swiftly began to move across the open ground.

More Long Knives? he wondered. KGB?

Bolan crouched behind a tree at the side of the trail. When lightning winked, he spotted the body of the Long Knife, glimpsed the mangled leg snared in the bear trap.

But it wasn't the steel jaws that had killed the Long Knife.

Bolan stood, decided to check the dead man when he heard something thunk beside him.

Whirling, Bolan raked the shadows with the M-16, searching for a target.

He found nothing.

Except the severed head of the Long Knife near his feet.

Then a tall shadow slid out of the woods, a hundred feet beside Bolan.

Lightning washed over the dark figure of Lev Belokai.

Bolan saw the grin stretch the lips on that ghoul's face, a gaunt death's head behind the steaming downpour.

KGB.

Terror and murder in the flesh.

Bolan felt his finger tighten around the M-16's trigger.

2

Two of a kind.

Death incarnate.

In the teeming downpour, gripped in the raging thunderstorm, the Executioner and the KGB assassin stood splay-legged like two Old West gunfighters.

Blood from Belokai's kill dripped off the Kukri blade. Bolan clutched the lowered M-16 at his side.

The Executioner knew he should have killed this butcher where he stood, but something locked in Bolan's mind. For a second he thought he saw his alter ego in the shadowed face of the KGB killer. A man wedded to Death, like himself. But a killing machine from the other side.

The Iron Curtain.

KGB.

The enemy.

Yeah, the Executioner thought, two of a kind. But entities created at the farthest spectrum of the universe. Soldiers now facing each other down on different sides of the gates of hell.

"Executioner," Belokai said, his gaze narrowing as the rain lashed his face, his accent thick. "I know who you are. But this is not the time for us. It must wait. I can see in your eyes that you understand this. We shall meet again. Soon. In a very cold place." He pointed toward the cabin with the Kukri. "They are all dead. There is no defector. Like you, I feel Death. It is there." Then he motioned toward the trail with the blade. "Like him, Executioner," he said, drawing the tip of the Kukri across his neck. "Your head next."

Lightning flashed, and Bolan met Belokai's stare.

Like a turkey, Bolan thought, lifting the M-16 to end it at that moment. Thanksgiving's going to come a little early this year, guy.

But when lightning sheeted again, the Executioner saw only darkness where the assassin had stood. Bolan searched the forest gloom, but there was no sign of the KGB killer. Not a shadow. Not even a rustle of brush.

There was only the wind, the rain and the darkness.

Briefly, Bolan thought about what the Russian had said. It sounded as if the assassin wanted to turn the mission into some sort of game. The hunter and the hunted. Search and destroy. In a way, though, that was how the KGB and the CIA operated. It *was* a game. A game of life and death, with the world the stage, and the nations of the world, NATO, Warsaw Pact, Third World, hanging in the balance on the fulcrum of nuclear annihilation. The Russian mind loved intrigue, suspense, Bolan knew. The Soviets were suspicious of everyone, including their own people. Russia was a land ruled by terror and force. Always had been. Always would be.

Bolan had been there. He had seen it firsthand when he'd penetrated Dzerzhinsky Square in the heart of Moscow to hunt and kill Greb Strakhov, the man responsible for the death of his woman, April Rose.

Nothing had really changed since then. The Iron Curtain killers still wanted the head of Mack Bolan.

The KGB, Bolan thought, as he moved back toward the death house. A secret police army much like the Gestapo, founded and organized by Felix Dzerzhinsky to help Lenin bolster his power, entrench the Russian masses firmly in Lenin's reign of terror. Except that, unlike Hitler's evil vision of a thousand-year Reich, the KGB's international murder squad lived on in the flesh to spread its poison across the globe.

Propaganda, murder, corruption and terrorism were synonymous with the Committee for State Security. Assassination, sabotage, kidnapping and extortion spelled KGB. No, Bolan knew, it wasn't the bulk of the Russian masses who were the enemy of the world. It was the elite of the state, the ones who lived the good life, who kept those masses under the thumb of Big Brother. They were the enemy. They were the hydra reaching out with cancerous tentacles to strangle what was left of the free world.

KGB. Mafia. Palestine Liberation Organization. Nazi Germany. It was all the same force. Animal man out to take, conquer and destroy. Animal man driven by the dark side of his nature.

It was war everlasting, yeah, Bolan knew. There would always be an enemy. There would always be animal man.

Inside the cabin, Bolan found Marchetti where he'd left him. But the SOD man was fast losing his hold on life. The light in the operative's eyes faded in and out, flickering like candlelight.

As the Executioner crouched over the SOD man, Marchetti suddenly said, "The Company doesn't forget that easily, Bolan...or forgive."

The revelation didn't surprise the Executioner. "Okay, so now you know who you're talking with."

A strangled laugh sounded in Marchetti's throat. "Yeah...I had a feeling I knew the moment you broke that door down, guns blazing.... What is it now? What crusade have you taken up? Some damned good agents died the last time you blew through town...."

"That's an old bone, Marchetti. I never took out any of your people. Unless they were dirty."

The SOD man coughed up blood. "What the hell do you want, Bolan? You come to get caught up in the war?"

"Is that what this is, Marchetti? A war between the CIA and the KGB?"

Another choked laugh. "C'mon, Bolan, the war's been going on for years. It only keeps escalating. Forget the cold war garbage, but you probably already understand that. Why should I help you?"

"Maybe to save some lives, Marchetti."

The CIA man searched the ice-blue eyes above him, appeared deep in thought for a long moment.

"Where's Baknov?" the Executioner pushed. "Look, Marchetti, I know the trade-off is set to go down in Alaska, I just don't know where."

Surprise flashed through Marchetti's eyes. "You've got some pretty good intel back in D.C. Mind if I ask who?"

"Yeah," the Executioner said abruptly. "Baknov, Marchetti. The trade-off."

"Hell, there is no trade-off." Marchetti hacked up blood, his eyes rolling back in his head. "I'm dying, Bolan...."

"Then help your guys, Marchetti. Help our side. Talk."

"We suspected ... the KGB was planning a double-cross."

"Is that the reason for the bear traps around the perimeter?"

Marchetti nodded weakly. "We want Snipes and Dover back; they want their guy. Neither side is going to back down in this. You see, neither side can really go at each other like we want...because of the bomb. What really goes on between us and the ComBloc countries never gets printed. Hell, the CIA doesn't dare do what you've done to their guys. We're handcuffed by the press, the National Security Council ... the Senate Intelligence Committee. All the suits that aren't there in the field. Sons of bitches calling the shots from behind the safety of a desk. Hell, you were in Nam. You know how that action goes.''

Bolan knew, all right. But the best soldier, he believed, was apolitical. Still, it was always the soldier who had to clean up the mess. The cleanup was called war.

''What I'm trying to tell you is that the Company damned your every move. Let me tell you, a lot of those guys were just green with fucking envy. Yeah, a lot of the boys at Langley and Peary would rather be renegade like you. It would be a goddamn lot easier most of the time.

''But the Company can hardly make a move without getting muddied, without the yellow journalists smearing shit all over our faces. The press never tells the American people how many peasant villages get razed, how many people are slaughtered in Central and South America by the Communist guerrillas. No one ever hears about the tens of thousands of Afghans dying because the Russians are spraying nerve gas over their country.

''You just hear about the Company's dirty tricks, like we're supposed to be playing fucking footsie with the Communist bastards while the Russians are sweeping up half the globe with the hammer and sickle. We don't always make the best, or even the right decisions . . . but that's the price tag attached to keeping back the Communists. Someone's always going to suffer.''

Bolan understood fully the war between Uncle Sam and the Soviet Union. Moscow was, without a doubt, attempting to perch itself right in America's backyard with a Central American takeover. Marchetti was dying on Bolan's hands, but the agent seemed to gain a new strength, fight off the inevitable as bitter resentment over things he could never change came to his mind. Bolan was losing patience.

"I don't have the time, guy. You don't, either. The point."

"The point is, Bolan..." Marchetti coughed up more blood. "The point is there are people behind the scenes pulling for you. Myself included."

"Tell me about the war between the CIA and the KGB? Is Baknov for real? Where's this master list?"

"B-Baknov," the CIA op said snorting. "We...we don't know. He could be a dangle operative. He was a high-ranking officer with the KGB before he bolted. He's been under heavy guard since he got here three weeks ago. Truth serum...hours of interrogation. Claims the master list is on microfilm. Somewhere in a Christian village in Damascus. If he's a dangle, then he's been brainwashed damned good by Big Brother. We haven't broken him yet.

"The safehouse here was just a decoy. Yeah, we knew the KGB would send a goon squad after him. A topflight goon with the KGB's Thirteenth Section doesn't just blow the country without bringing down the anger of *Otdel 9*. Right now, a team of specialists is holding Baknov in a town...Lee's Crossing. It's about thirty klicks west of here. It's a tough coal-mining town. The team is holed up in a hotel-type saloon there. Christ...if the KGB wanted them, they wouldn't have any trouble spotting our guys there.

"But we're not trying to hide from them, Bolan. Both sides want blood. Both sides want it all. Alaska's been declared the battleground. A test of strength. A test of wills."

It made sense to Bolan. All-out combat. Winner take all. With the stakes being the lives of the other side's defectors. And all the chips the three spies.

With a wild card of vengeance thrown into the deck.

Marchetti's eyes rolled back in his head as he spit up more blood. "Black dice, Bolan...it was in all our eyes this time. I can see it in your eyes, too. You've been out in the field too long...that's what black dice means. Means an agent's been under fire too long...had one too many close brushes with death. Means the luck of the draw has run out on him. A guy with experience like that can see death in another man's eyes.... Yeah, the next time the dice of chance roll, they'll roll up black. Death. You're the lone crapshooter now, Bolan. Black dice...is in your eyes."

Bolan's gaze narrowed.

A death rattle rasped past Marchetti's lips.

The wind seemed to howl with a sudden fierceness around Mack Bolan.

Black dice, the lone warrior thought.

The dice of death.

The black dice were already rolling.

The players had gathered.

And the losers in this game would be the dead.

Gently, Bolan brushed Marchetti's eyelids shut.

Then let the dice roll, soldier, the Executioner thought as he stood. I'll take what I get.

A rumble stirred in the pit of Bolan's gut. War-honed instinct warned him that a nightmare, a blood-bath unlike anything he had yet experienced, had just begun.

It was a feeling he couldn't shake.

JACK GRIMALDI, ACE PILOT, long-time ally and close friend of Mack Bolan, waited out the storm in the cockpit of a Bell jet turbine chopper. The Huey, on loan from Stony Man Farm, boasted 5.56 mm mini-guns and 40 mm cannons mounted externally on turrets.

But Jack Grimaldi was anything but "on loan" to the Executioner. He had been called in by the big guy while soaking up the rays in Honolulu. R and R, he thought. Right now, it was out of the frying pan and into the fire.

Something big was cooking under the black turbulent sky. Something ugly. Grimaldi had been briefed by Bolan on the situation. Defectors. Trade-off. KGB and CIA. Both men had known the numbers before setting down in the clearing along the Virginia-West Virginia border. The Bell carried all the necessary combat gear for the Executioner's latest battle, in a crate in the fuselage. This time out, Grimaldi knew, it looked as if they were headed for Alaska. The last frontier.

Grimaldi had been with Bolan all the way, from the start, right through the big guy's blitzkrieg campaigns against the Mafia, then during the government-sanctioned terrorist wars. He'd seen the Mafia-scorching Bolan "die," only to be reborn as Colonel John Macklin Phoenix.

Those days were gone.

The Executioner was on his own again. Just the way Striker wanted it. No, Grimaldi corrected himself, the *only* way it should be.

But, at the moment, Grimaldi wondered where the big guy was. The CIA safehouse was fifteen kilometers north. The Soviet defector, Baknov, was supposed to be under heavy guard there. The night warrior had left the Bell more than three hours ago at 2035. A soft probe, then a rendezvous back at the LZ. Grimaldi had been told to sit tight at the landing zone, wait for further orders.

Hell, a soft probe had a way of going hard in a lightning flash where Mack Bolan was concerned, Grimaldi knew.

He scoffed at himself for worrying. He peered out through the thick Plexiglass, wind and golfball-size raindrops hammering the cockpit bubble. They would have to wait out the storm anyway. A rotary-winged bird was tricky to fly even under the best of conditions, even with the best navigator at the helm.

Grimaldi folded his arms over his chest. He hated just killing time, but orders were orders. Bolan knew what he was doing. That was something Grimaldi would never doubt.

He felt the wind shake the Bell. He heard the rain pounding the chopper's hull. The sound of the storm's fury seemed to massage his tired frame. His mind drifted off into sleep.

They came out of the night.

Grimaldi snapped awake as he felt the wind and the rain wash over him. Jerking his head sideways, he found himself staring at the barrels of two M-16s. At least a dozen shadows surrounded the Bell.

"Out of the chopper, boy."

Grimaldi stared at the big, bearded man in the leather flight-style jacket. As lightning flashed, he glimpsed the others in the group. Long, rain-matted hair. Denim or leather jackets. Beards and wild, angry eyes.

"Who the hell are you people?" Grimaldi growled.

Art "Weeb" Jordan reached a long arm across the cockpit, grabbed Grimaldi and snatched the pilot out of the Bell.

Grimaldi saw stars as his head struck the edge of the doorway. Then he felt his face hit the wet grass. A boot impacted on his guts, drove the wind from his lungs. It happened so fast, there'd been no time to react. What the hell was going on, he wondered, reaching for his holstered .45 Colt ACP.

"He's got a gun, Weebie!"

"Freeze it right there, boy! Or your ass is ours!"

Grimaldi froze. He looked up, eyes slitted against the downpour. The shadows circled him. The ugly snouts of M-16s stared him down.

"We just came from that CIA safehouse," Jordan growled. "Seven of our guys bought the farm. I ain't talkin' about Camp Peary neither."

"And just who are you heroes?" Grimaldi rasped.

"Don't get smart, asshole!" the pilot heard one of the others snarl.

"We're the Long Knives," Weeb Jordan told Grimaldi. "And we don't like it when outsiders come trespassing on our turf. Somebody snuffed our people. Even chopped one of our probate's heads off with a goddamned machete. I'm asking you once—who are you?"

Grimaldi knew there was no point in lying. These jerks meant to kill him. Still, even the truth would be hard to swallow.

"We're free-lance soldiers," Grimaldi answered.

"Bullshit," Jordan growled. "This is an Army chopper. I was in Nam, boy. I flew these gunships at Soc Trang in '69 and '70. Those are fucking miniguns and 40-millimeter cannons. You're Special Forces, right?" He drilled a boot in Grimaldi's side.

"Whatever you say, dumbass," Grimaldi shot back through gritted teeth. "You believe what you want."

Jordan sneered. "You think we're just a bunch of stupid crackers, don't ya? You got some kind of hotshot operation going on here, and you're covering somebody's ass. Pick him up!'' he ordered his companions.

As three Long Knives hauled Grimaldi to his feet, Jordan jammed the barrel of his M-16 under the ace pilot's jaw. Another gang member stripped the prisoner of his Colt .45, while another patted Grimaldi down.

"He's clean, Weebie."

"Yeah, you're clean," Jordan said. "You'll be dead, though, you don't spill your guts to Freeman. Move him out!''

The Long Knives shoved Grimaldi ahead.

The rain pounded the Executioner's ace pilot.

But the real storm, Grimaldi thought, had yet to be unleashed.

Mack Bolan would return.

3

They were peasants.

Amerikanski peasants. They were the best kind, Belokai thought, as he sliced off another strip of cheese with the Kukri. *Da,* Russia had always been a land of peasants, but the peasants of the motherland, Belokai knew, accepted their lot. They had to. In America it was different. There was a huge gap between the haves, he thought, and the have-nots. He recalled the expression, which he had heard for the first time in a bar in the coal-mining town just yesterday during an argument between peasant coal miners who had been out of work for six months. Haves. Have-nots. He liked that. It described the injustice and inequality of the western world.

The economic gap between the haves and the have-nots might as well have spanned the globe, Belokai thought. A gap that was a million miles wide, that would never be bridged. The have-nots resented the haves. Hated them. If an *Amerikanski* was not rich in money, then he was led to believe he was worthless. By the media. By his own people. There was an imbalance, a great injustice somewhere in the capitalist system, Belokai decided.

He looked around the shack. Pots, tin cans, cheap oil paintings depicting deserts and sunsets hung from pegs along the wall. A fire burned in the cast-iron potbellied stove beside a chipped, rusty sink. *Da,* these peasants had to go outside, walk almost a kilometer just to draw water from a well.

He took in the wooden floor of the shack, barren except for a mud-stained brown rug near the front door. Kerosene lanterns, hung from the ceiling, flickered a pale orange light over the haggard, hollow-eyed, dirt-grimed, tear-streaked faces of the woman, her two teenage daughters and her nine-year-old son. Belokai had been told that the electricity and the telephone had been turned off because the husband hadn't worked in ten months. No work, no rubles, the KGB assassin thought. No electricity. Nothing. They were poor, filthy, despicable creatures. But the capitalist system was despicable.

In Russia it was different. There was always work for the peasants. In Russia men were not allowed to complain about their lot. Unless, of course, they longed for a gulag vacation in Siberia. Here, though, Belokai heard nothing but complaints. Against the government. Against the unions. Against the family. Against the worker. Against each other.

Nyet, all was not well with the great capitalist system. In Russia the people were looked after, cared for by Moscow. Or so Belokai had been told. It was more than twenty years since he'd left that farming village in the Urals. He tended to forget his peasant origins; indeed, the mere thought of his childhood in the Urals was repulsive.

Now, he was a hero in the KGB. Destiny had called him. Fate had rewarded him for his heroic service to the motherland. And the KGB had been good to him. He was one of the elite, and how the rest of Russia lived was of little concern to him. He knew the Russian people had grown restless with their lot, but the Kremlin was becoming just as concerned about the satellite countries. A major revolt was feared.

There was a rumble of discontent going through all of the Warsaw Pact countries. Worse, West German intelligence officers had been discovered moving in and out of East Germany, infiltrating the East German Secret Service. An underground movement for German unification was now under way in East Berlin, but the KGB had come up with no names of German criminals yet.

And the German problem, Belokai knew, would always be with Russia. Germany was now a sleeping dog. Moscow believed that there was a great chance World War III would begin when East and West Germany sought to unite. That could happen sooner than either Moscow or Washington was aware of. Even though the German youth were very antimilitary, Belokai knew that was apt to change overnight. Particularly if there were major uprisings in the satellite countries. *Da*, there were many lessons to be learned from history. The Russians had learned them from their terrible, and terrifying experience with the *nemetski*, the speakers of gibberish, in World War I and the Great Patriotic War. There was far more to fear from the Germans than the Americans, Germany would someday march. Again.

The Germans were not to be trusted.

And many Americans, Belokai knew, were of German descent. That, he thought, was hard to believe. America was a vulgar, uncultured, barbaric land. Most Americans were just bitter, ignorant, spiteful peasants, and it was hard to believe they were of Teutonic, Frankish or Gothic blood.

Belokai chomped down on the slice of cheese. He looked at the woman and her children. They were frightened. Better still, they were terrified of him.

"What are you going to do to us?" the woman asked.

A thin smile slashed Belokai's lips. It was the fourth time during the past hour the peasant woman had asked him that. Belokai checked his watch, then looked at Dmitry Dmivsky, who guarded the door.

"I tell you that I have still not decided," Belokai answered. "All depends on your husband and what my men find out in your town. Do not worry, dear lady," the KGB assassin said. He smiled and took another bite of the cheese. "Whatever it is I decide...it will not be good. For you."

Belokai liked that answer. Dmivsky obviously liked it, too; he chuckled.

For a moment, Belokai thought that he should have been still living in a dacha along the Black Sea. Retirement had been short-lived. Baknov, one-time friend and KGB associate of Belokai, had turned criminal. During the early seventies, he and Baknov had penetrated the British MI5. Indeed, Belokai knew, behind the scenes Britain belonged to Moscow. Thanks largely to the espionage and sabotage of himself and Baknov. But all the work the two of them had done against NATO was jeopardized when Baknov defected from Britain to America.

And the Thirteenth Section of the KGB had called Belokai out of retirement.

His orders from the Kremlin were clear: capture and bring Baknov back to Moscow, or eliminate the great traitor. At any cost. *Otdel 9* had even granted Belokai the privilege of killing as many CIA agents, indeed, as many Americans as he saw necessary in order to complete the task.

Suddenly light stabbed through the window near the front door.

Belokai watched as his men returned with the coal miner in the peasant's pickup truck.

"Daddy!" one of the girls cried.

"Silence!" Belokai rasped, as he stood up.

The front door opened, and a short, burly, black-bearded man in a lumberjack coat and wool cap was ushered through the doorway by three of Belokai's men. Belokai watched as the father tried to break free from the clutches of Gleb Chaadeyev's massive fists.

Chaadeyev, towering over the American by a foot, chopped the coal miner over the head with the butt of his Makarov. Belokai smiled as the American dropped to his knees.

"Report," Belokai ordered.

"They are holding Baknov in what the Americans call a hotel barroom in the town. He," Chaadeyev said, nodding down at the coal miner, "went into the bar. He saw them. He identified them. We are ready to move on them. Whenever you see fit, tovarich."

The coal miner, his hand wrapped over the back of his head, looked up at Belokai. There was hatred and fear in the man's stare. "I've done what you asked. Now let my family go."

One of the teenage girls began to sob.

Belokai looked at each of the four Americans. His smile widened, and his eyes appeared to grow colder.

The storm raged on outside.

Belokai hefted the Kukri in his hand. He held the knife up to his face, the 22½-inch blade mirroring the wavering orange kerosene light.

The coal miner knew. Belokai could clearly read the horror of the realization in the American's eyes.

"No," the man pleaded. "Look, Russian, damn you! I did your spying!" Terror crept into the coal miner's voice as he looked imploringly from the faces of his wife and children to the cold gray eyes of Belokai. "At least let them go."

Chaadeyev and Dmivsky grabbed the man, dragged him on his knees across the floor.

"No!" the coal miner's wife cried as Chaadeyev thrust her husband's head down on the table.

Belokai lifted the Kukri.

The coal miner struggled.

"Stay still, or watch your wife and children die!" Chaadeyev struggled.

The woman buried the faces of her children against her bosom.

Bolan, Belokai thought, lifting the Kukri higher over his head, his gaze fixed on the back of the man's neck. Soon the head bent under the knife would be that of the feared and hated Executioner. Next. The great American warrior, who struck terror right into the heart of Moscow. Bolan, who was nothing but a Pole. Bolan, whose head would be Belokai's trophy to take back to the Kremlin.

A violent trembling overcame Belokai. His face flushed as a terrible wrath suddenly filled him.

The flickering kerosene light cast a grim shadow on the cabin's wall, playing out the grisly scene of death.

IN THE DEAD OF NIGHT, Lee's Crossing looked like a ghost town to Mack Bolan. The Executioner steered the four-wheel drive Ford pickup down the steep one-lane asphalt road toward the coal-mining settlement. The truck was an unexpected gift from the Company. Dead men don't drive, Bolan thought, and sensed that the night was still very much alive with the presence of Death.

Was Death friend or foe, the Executioner wondered. Over the years it had been both, at times conspiring against him, at others cooperating with the warrior. Death was neutral, he decided.

Bolan parked the pickup at the far east end of town, opting for a quick surveillance of the wide paved street and the two-dozen wood or red brick buildings. With a black windbreaker concealing Big Thunder, the man in combat blacksuit stepped out into the night. A blast of wind chilled the soldier, but the rain had diminished to a fine drizzle.

There was no sign of life on the street, but Bolan heard the muted laughter, conversation and clack of billiard balls toward the west end of town. There, perhaps a dozen late-fifties-model cars and trucks were parked. Along with four Harley hawgs. High, wooded hills surrounded the town, and lights burned in the windows of box-shaped homes clinging to the slopes. The silhouettes of two water towers loomed in the distance. Rusted automobile hulks littered the town's perimeter. Hard-luck city all the way, Bolan thought. Small-town America—the dinosaur of the twentieth century. Yeah, the country was changing, all right. Sometimes, he couldn't help but wonder if it was for the better or the worse.

Bolan stepped up onto the boardwalk, headed in the direction of the saloon. Ahead, light spilled from a large plate-glass window.

A saloon in a dying West Virginia coal-mining town. Leave it to the CIA to pick a hole-up spot. But often the best cover was the least cover. The CIA safehouse was proof enough that inconspicuous was often the undoing of an operation.

Bolan stepped toward the light.

He was about to set foot in a den of vipers.

LEV BELOKAI LOWERED the infrared binoculars. "Bolan," he muttered, then smiled. This was good, he thought. No, this was perfect. The battle had already begun. Still, Belokai couldn't, didn't want to believe all those stories about the fearsome Executioner.

From his vantage point in the hills high above the town to the south, Belokai gave Lee's Crossing one final recon. The town seemed deserted except for the activity at the tavern. And there, he saw, was where the Executioner was headed.

The Russian gave his four-man killteam a final look. Arkady Levin. Pasha Kivev. Ivan Pavlovich. Pytor Drozdov. Hard-eyed. Grim-faced. Tight-lipped. Levin and Kivev both toted Argentine versions of the 7.65 mm Mannlicher. An accurate pistol with big muzzle velocity. Pavlovich carried the heavy firepower—a Czech M-25 subgun. Drozdov would storm the tavern from the back with an AK-47. *Da,* Belokai thought, this was war. And if he was sending his men to be sacrificed at the hands of the Executioner, then only he would have to live with that knowledge. The best assassin was only as good as his adversary.

A man was only as strong as his harshest test in life.

During a killhunt the professional always exercised patience. Skill was useless without careful thought, without foresight. From experience, the professional learned to bide his time. He studied his prey, learned the target's strengths and weaknesses. Patience, timing and execution. The true assassin knew how to use them, and always did. Survival, victory depended on them alone. Luck was for the amateur.

More than anything else, Belokai now wanted the head of Mack Bolan.

The KGB killer turned, looked at the two shadows behind him. Dmivsky and Chaadeyev. Good men. Good agents. But they were young, with little experience. They had not killed the hundreds of enemies of the state that he had over the years of his unfailing service to the motherland.

But they followed his orders without question. Doubt was something that didn't have to be verbalized. Belokai prided himself on being able to read men. Eyes spoke thoughts, if a man knew what to look for.

"Go, comrades," Belokai ordered his men. "You know what to do."

The four-man assassination squad moved down the slope.

Belokai nodded in satisfaction. His killteam knew what to do.

Kill anything and everything.

But Mack Bolan had once again entered the picture.

Anything could happen now, Belokai thought.

He suspected the worst, that his men would die.

But he would be one step closer to his *glavni protiv-nik*—his principal target. If there was a weakness in the Executioner, then Belokai would find that weakness and use it against Bolan.

And Belokai believed the principal target would be his for the slaughter.

But the time was not yet right.

Fate was on his side.

Fate would drop the head of Mack Bolan right into his lap.

A thin smile slitted the KGB killer's lips as he lifted the field glasses to his eyes.

4

Bolan spotted them right away.

He couldn't miss the three-man team of Company specialists and their Soviet defector. They could have been Boers in a black township in South Africa. They could have been Bedouins riding on camelback through Bel Air. They could have been Masai warriors walking the streets of downtown Nairobi.

They were exactly what they looked like, and everybody in that room knew they were government issue.

Bolan figured there was only one reason why the CIA was playing this deadly game right out in the open—they wanted to kick the KGB's ass clear back to 2 Dzerzhinsky Square. And they were making no bones about it.

Yeah, the vultures were gathering. A feast of international flesh. Open war. Not a goddamn DMZ to be found.

Let those dice roll.

Bolan stood inside the door of the saloon, took in the scene at a glance. Redneck city. The barroom was something out of Tombstone, circa 1870s. Long,

shiny-top mahogany bar with wooden stools and brass
foot-rail. Circular wooden tables clustered around the
large room. Sawdust on the floor soaking up beer,
puke and, probably more often than not, a little
blood. Three pool tables sat near the back. There, a
dozen bearded longhairs in denim and leather jackets
swilled brew and liquor, shot pool and shot the bull.

Conversation stopped momentarily when Bolan
entered the saloon, and all eyes looked his way. The air
was heavy with danger. Bolan could smell it. In small-
town U.S.A. a stranger wasn't exactly greeted with
open arms. But then again neither was the neighbor-
hood leper. Outsiders usually brought bad news,
trouble or both. These people were still living in the
nineteenth century.

The room was packed with local toughs, six bikers
with the colors of the Blood Eagles and an assortment of townies—old-timers mostly, who'd been
kicked in the teeth more than once by Lady Luck.

A den of vipers. A nest of vultures. A vat of blood-
suckers.

Mack Bolan walked right into the heart of danger.

The team of specialists was seated at a round table
behind the end of the bar. From the way they looked
at him, Bolan knew they expected bad news, or trouble. The Executioner had come to bring them both.
This was not a night of choices.

Two good ol' boys with bellies that would have
made a sumo wrestler weep with envy sat at the bar.
Along with the rest of the mob, they eyeballed Bolan.

But it was the flash of metal pinned to the chests of the two good ol' boys that caught Bolan's attention for an instant. Law. That was all this night needed. Beer-swilling good-ol'-boy lawmen caught in a cross fire hurricane. Bolan put them out of his mind.

The rest of the room didn't forget Bolan as easily. Conversation picked up again, but it was muted by a suspicious and hostile undercurrent. Patrons at the bar watched Bolan's reflection in the mirror that ran the length of the bar behind the stacked shelves of bottles.

Bolan quickly saw that the beautiful people in that fine establishment felt much the same way about the government issue as they did about him. The room was full of hard-luckers, for damned sure, but their luck might just turn a whole lot harder if they tried to interfere in his business.

The soldier walked up to the table of specialists. He stood there and purposely drew out the tension. The threat of danger and violence often had a way of making hard-nosed Company types feel at ease.

Around him, Bolan heard activity pick up. Spittoons clanged. Pool balls clacked. Fingers riffled card edges. A country and western song about a one-legged hillbilly from Missouri who'd just shot and killed his fat nag of a wife, Mabel, twanged through the saloon. Bolan smelled the sweat, the smoke and the fear in the air.

This was one long night, he thought, that was going to get a lot longer. And a whole lot hotter.

The Executioner looked at the three SOD men. All clean-cut, middle to late thirties. Windbreakers and slacks. And the ever-present bulge of a piece beneath their jackets. Warily they appraised Bolan.

The Soviet defector, Baknov, was a short, thickset Russian. Fear showed in his dark, bloodshot eyes. The SOD people, Bolan could tell, had put the Russian through one tough ringer of an interrogation. But that was standard for either side. Brutality and treachery played no favorites.

The espionage world of the CIA and KGB was a complex game, much like a maze. Their world lived, indeed, thrived on cunning entrapments, agents provocateurs, spies and counterspies, double- and triple-crosses. Of course the KGB had greater flexibility and freedom to operate. Terror states usually granted that privilege to its intelligence people. In fact, the KGB was the most powerful, brutal and efficient intelligence network the world had ever seen.

In the States it was, sadly, very different with the CIA. Thanks largely to the bleeding hearts in the press, and the desk-lifers in D.C. who called the shots from the safety of an office and couldn't bear to think that the guys in the white hats had to operate as down-and-dirty ugly as the guys in the black hats.

Sure, Bolan knew, the CIA had its hands cuffed by the very system it was designed to protect. And at one time that same system had sought desperately to get Bolan to play by its rules. Unfortunately, the cannibals of the world never recognized those rules. Mack

Bolan couldn't recognize those rules, either. He had to fight the savages with their own fire. Uncle Sam had sought to control the Bolan hellfire with the Stony Man antiterrorist operations. It didn't work.

"Colonel John Phoenix," the big SOD operative next to Baknov said, his tone somber, his look dark. "Or I should say, Mack Bolan, the Executioner."

"You people sure have a thing about burned bridges, don't you," Bolan returned.

"I thought the Stony Man days were over," the big operative went on. "But, of course, I almost forgot. You're on your own again. What do you want?"

"I want in."

The agent scoffed, looked at his SOD colleagues and smiled. "What you want, Bolan, and what you're going to get are two different things. Don't come fucking around in this or you'll regret it."

Bolan let the threat pass for the moment. "I think you may be the one who starts having regrets. Your decoy people are dead. All of them."

The SOD men drew rigid with tension.

"They were hit by a group of Jim Crow patriots called the Long Knives," Bolan informed them. As he said it, he noticed the table of denim-clad townies next to him look his way.

The big op bared his teeth. "Christ," he rasped under his breath. Then he looked at Bolan, hard-eyed. "And you just happened to stumble in on the hit, right?"

"Listen, it doesn't matter how I know about this trade-off. The fact is, I know. You're holding a human time bomb here," Bolan said, indicating Baknov. "You want our people back. They're in Alaska. And Marchetti told me there's a war set to take place there between the CIA and the KGB. One man stands a much better chance of penetrating the KGB's defenses in Alaska and getting those intelligence officers back. Not some CIA paramilitary strike force."

"Let me tell you something, hotshot," the operative said, jabbing a finger at Bolan, "we're not sitting at some conference table with the KGB here. They don't want any bargain. We're not looking to bargain, either. This is war. No deal, Bolan. You're not in. In fact, you're on your way out. You interfere in this search and destroy, you'll be back at the top of our hit list. Am I making myself clear?"

Ice froze in Bolan's eyes. "No, I think I'm the one who's not making himself clear. Your numbers are dwindling fast. I think you're going to need all the fire support you can get."

"Bull . . ."

Suddenly, the big operative froze. He looked past Bolan, fear stark in his eyes.

Instantly, the Executioner became aware of the leaden hush that dropped over the crowd.

A flurry of motion tore through the barroom.

Chair legs scraped, and Bolan saw the back door near the bathroom flung wide open with a crash.

The three KGB assassins spread out near the front. They opened up with the Mannlicher pistols and M-25s. Indiscriminately, they slaughtered ten patrons in the opening split seconds of the hit. Targets were random and everywhere. ComBloc lead punched open skulls, split faces. Screams ripped through the saloon. Blood splashed the walls.

One of the SOD operatives hurled the table on its side. All three Company men dived for the floor. Bolan glimpsed an AK-47 blazing from the blackness of the back doorway. He snatched Baknov away from the SOD men, flung the Soviet defector behind the bar. Behind Bolan, a hail of 7.62 mm hornets rained over the SOD men.

Diving, Bolan reached cover behind the bar an instant before hot lead chewed up the front of the counter. Slugs whined off brass, shattered glass, pulverized the bar mirror. Crouched, Bolan unholstered Big Thunder, then moved along the rear of the bar. Ahead, he saw the bartender corkscrew, arms windmilling, shattering bottles as the back of his skull cracked open under a hail of 9 mm and 7.65 mm slugs.

A Blood Eagle lunged for Drozdov. That mistake cost the would-be hero his life. Drozdov whirled, slammed the AK's muzzle into the biker's stomach. Blood, cloth, bone and organs erupted from the one-percenter's back. Gore splattered the other patrons nosediving to the sawdust behind the dead Blood Eagle. Drozdov continued to rake the area where the billiard tables stood, drilling other bikers and splintering the racks of cues.

Bolan rose over the counter. He added to the blistering roar of gunfire, the screams of terror and agony. Big Thunder cannoned three times, took out three of the four principal targets.

A 240-grain boattail slug tunneled out the chest of Pasha Kivev, hurling him through the plate-glass window.

Beside Bolan, the two lawmen were cut to shreds against the bar by ComBloc lead. Blood washed over the Executioner's face while liquor leaked out of shattered bottles behind him. As the AK-47 swung his way, he ducked, didn't see the results of his killshots against Arkady Levin and Ivan Pavlovich.

More bottles exploded like land mines above and behind Bolan as he moved behind the bar toward Baknov. The Russian defector was cowering there, shielding his head with his arms. Two of the three SOD men were not so lucky. Lifeless eyes stared at Bolan from beneath the splintered wood of the table, and arms and legs twitched in death throes. The big operative who had spoken to Bolan now scrabbled through the sawdust for a stainless Colt .45.

Bolan ended the fierce firefight.

As the tracking line of fire swept the bar beyond him, the Executioner lurched up over the counter. For a millisecond he met the wild-eyed gaze of Drozdov. The Russian realized his error in spraying an area where he thought the target should have, but had not, been.

Bolan blew the KGB butcher out into the night.

Quickly, Bolan took in the slaughterbed.

Bloodied, bullet-riddled bodies littered the floor, draped over the pool tables. Everything had been shot to hell within just seconds. Blood dripped out of perforated, twitching flesh, soaked up by the sawdust. Smoke curled from the ruins of the jukebox.

Bolan moved out from behind the bar, combat boots crunching glass slivers.

The pungent smell of liquor and the coppery odor of blood hung heavy in the air.

The Executioner saw some of the denim-clad local survivors stir to life. He took a step toward the pool tables, turned and glanced back at the big SOD operative. The Company man hauled himself to his feet. Not a scratch on the guy, Bolan noticed. The table and the bodies of his specialist buddies had shielded him from the initial AK volley.

Some guys had all the luck, Bolan thought.

But Lady Luck had been anything but kind to the majority in the barroom.

And Lady Luck sent another hard-lucker Bolan's way. Whether out of panic or just blind rage over the slaughter of his buddies, a Blood Eagle leaped to his feet, charged the lone man in blacksuit standing between the tables.

Bolan reacted instinctively. The Executioner pistoned a side kick into the biker's gut, almost driving the man's intestines into his spine as he slammed into the wall.

None of the other few survivors made a move on Bolan.

The SOD man looked at his buddies, then turned a slightly dazed look on Bolan. The Colt trembled in his hand. "Now what, hotshot?"

"Now we play ball," the Executioner grimly said.

"You think, huh."

Bolan let his piercing blue eyes lock on the SOD man for a moment.

"All right, all right," the specialist growled, then reached out a hand and snatched Baknov by the shoulder. "Go ahead," he growled at Bolan, shoving the Russian defector in front of the bar. "Lead the way."

Bolan didn't waste another second.

The KGB was on the march, and they were prowling for blood. Already the KGB had taken the lives of innocents and not-so-innocents, as well as the blood of the law and the lawless alike.

It was war, yeah, the Executioner knew.

And he intended to take the fire and the sword straight into the heart of the hammer and sickle.

LEV BELOKAI WAS PLEASED with the results. The murderous chaos below him was a sign of progress in his war against the Americans.

Bolan, the KGB colonel saw, led the great traitor and a CIA gangster away from the body of Pasha

Kivev, who had been dumped on the sidewalk just moments ago. Death always meant progress. The slaughter of his comrades had just proved to Belokai that he was pitted against a formidable foe. A prize certainly worth beheading.

At the moment, as Bolan and the others strode toward the truck, Belokai knew he could have taken the Dragunov sniper rifle out of the trunk of his rented car and dropped the feared Executioner, the great traitor and the gangster in their tracks. But that would have spoiled the hunt, made the war with the CIA much less memorable. *Nyet*. Belokai wanted to face Bolan down after his own execution squad had dismembered the CIA in Alaska. He wanted to strike fear into the Executioner's heart, to look him in the eye when he handed Bolan his own death.

And he wanted to take the traitor back to the Kremlin. Alive. *Da*, he wanted to personally see the KGB ship Baknov off to a Siberian concentration camp, to the gulag.

Terror was good only if there were examples from terror. Baknov had to be an example. Joseph Stalin, Belokai recalled, had been the perfect terror master. The rest of the world held Stalin accountable for some thirty million deaths. But Belokai knew it was closer to fifty million. He had been there. He had seen it. He had risen quickly in the ranks of Stalin's secret police. He had compiled the suspect lists. He had herded up thousands of traitors for the great one.

Indeed, the understanding of Mother Russia had only been made complete following the Great Patriotic War. Foot soldier Belokai had stood at arm's length from Stalin at Leningrad the day the trains packed with Russian prisoners had returned from the German camps in the Rhineland. Belokai had been waiting there for a brother who had been captured by the Nazis. Before going to that train station, Belokai had known what would become of those prisoners. But there had been a part of his mind that didn't want to believe it possible.

Until that train of prisoners rolled straight on through Leningrad to Siberia. Belokai had never seen nor heard of his brother again. But on that day he had come to understand what it meant to be a Russian. Strength. Pride. Relentlessness for the cause. *Da*, he understood why those trains had rolled on to Siberia. Any Russian who had allowed himself to be captured by the Nazis was not only suspect, but considered a coward, a traitor. There was no room in the motherland for weakness. Even flesh and blood, Belokai knew, was not above the greatness of the motherland.

Anyone could be sacrificed for the greater glory of Mother Russia.

As Belokai's four comrades had just been sacrificed.

Belokai turned, walked past Chaadeyev and Dmivsky. "Come, comrades," he said. "We go in hunt of bigger game."

5

"This thing could be bigger than either side wants to know about or acknowledge, Bolan," Special Operative James Kelly told the Executioner. "By big, I mean apocalyptic. By big, mister, I'm talking about World War III."

The back road through the hill country was pitch-black. As black as the mood in the CIA truck that Bolan had commandeered to take him back to the LZ and Jack Grimaldi.

Since leaving the carnage back at Lee's Crossing, Bolan hadn't learned any new information from Kelly about the Alaskan CIA-KGB war. But the big night-fighter now got the impression that Kelly was leading up to something. The Executioner gave the Company man free rein to talk.

"Bolan, Washington wants to put a stop to any of our people feeding the Soviets vital information. Once and for all. We've gotten the go-ahead from Langley to terminate all targets, principal and secondary. That means Snipes, Dover and all KGB personnel involved. They buy the goddamn farm, or it's our ass.

No courts. No press coverage. No martyrs for the bleeding-heart media.

"For the past ten years some of our people have been feeding the Russians information about ROBAT, that's the Robotic Obstacle Breeching Tank, the Joint Surveillance Target Attack Radar System, which most people know as JOINTSTARS, TACCS—Tactical Army Combat Service Support Computer System, and Pershing 2. They'd let their own country go under just so they can sit their fat ass down in some cottage on a scenic New England beach. Every Soviet counterpart," the Specialist said, glancing coldly at Baknov, who sat in stony silence between the SOD man and the Executioner, "was made thanks to some bastard on our side. Or because the KGB got counterintelligence people into key positions in our defense industries. But then again," the SOD man grumbled, seemingly as an afterthought, "the goddamn Russians have stolen every last piece of technology they own. First from the Germans, then Uncle Sam.

"It's a goddamned mess, and it seems to be getting worse. Hell, I could go on and on—SHORAD—a missile defence system, Binary Chemical Munitions, All Source Analysis System. All of the Army's top development projects. Close *and* Long Range Combat. Everything we now have, the Soviets have, too. And they got it because of our own people. I wouldn't be surprised if there's an inner circle of frigging traitors called the Benedict Arnold Club.

"And this so-called Strategic Defense Initiative? That the press jumped on and named after a goddamn kid's comic book movie? Thanks to an administration that couldn't keep its mouth shut because it was hungry for reelection. Hell, do you think the Soviets would ever advertise top-secret projects? I'll tell you this much, they've been working on killer satellites for fifteen years."

A thin smile slashed Baknov's lips.

Kelly caught the look on the Russian's face, scowled. "Yeah, look at this bastard. Just grinning. He knows. The Soviets beat us into space with Sputnik, and our handle here has already informed us that they'll beat us into space with their own SDI. In fact, we've already got a code name for their first killer space station," he snorted. "Medusa. And it'll probably turn everything we could ever throw at the Soviets and their satellite countries into just that—stone. Useless freaking junk."

"I'm still not quite following you, guy. What does any of this have to do with World War III?"

Kelly rubbed his jaw, stared out the window for a moment, lost in deep, dark thought.

"Everything, Bolan. But maybe nothing. You see, I know some very important, very influential people in Washington. People behind the scenes, but people who probably have more power in Washington than any thieving sons of bitches on the Hill. They're called special analysts. You know the type, the ones who sit in a think tank all day, every day. Well, these guys sit around drawing up war scenarios. They're the government's pretty boys. Big hotshot, all-knowing intelligentsia.

"Uncle Sam gives these people just about anything and everything they want. Well, these special analysts operate on a master computer called, appropriately enough, SOURCE. SOURCE is tied in to almost every computer system in the free world, the Third World and several of the Communist countries in Eastern Europe. Not even the Russians know about SOURCE. Yet. It's all done by satellite. Yeah, we've got a great big computer in the sky that's collecting intelligence behind the Iron Curtain. Let me ask you something, Bolan. What do you think might be the one greatest single fear the Russians have?"

Bolan shrugged. He could have given the SOD man twenty answers, any of which would have been correct. "Enlighten me."

"German reunification."

"It'll never happen," Bolan said.

"Bullshit." Kelly was grim, adamant. "That's what most people would say. That's what the Germans, namely the German intelligence wants the rest of the world to think.

"These special analysts claim that, in a very real sense, World War I is not over. If the world survives another two hundred years World War II will be recounted as a skirmish, merely phase two of the Great Twentieth-Century War. That war has just been suspended since '45. The think tanks believe the final confrontation will start in Europe, the area from the Baltic States to the Alps, called the Central Front. The East German border is Russia's frontier, their survival post against military threat. Okay, you've got the self-defense organizations of NATO and the Warsaw Pact. They both watch all of Europe. They both want all of Europe.''

"The East Bloc has already revolted, Kelly," Bolan pointed out. "The Hungarians. The Czechs. The Poles. The East Germans. All of them were put down right away by Russian force."

"Ah, yes, but here comes the catch. East Germany is Russia's strongest ally. Thus, they have the highest standard of living. Simply because the Russians fear the Germans more than anybody else, including the Americans. A reunified Germany would end up just like China within ten years. Armed to the teeth, and ready to march into Moscow.

"As of this moment there is an underground movement going through the ComBloc countries. The Russians, Bolan, as I'm sure you well know, create an atmosphere of malcontent and unrest by fomenting the troubles in that country. The CIA has now taken it upon itself to do the same in the East Bloc countries. Of course, we can't do it directly; we have counterintelligence operatives from those countries working from the inside."

"So," Bolan said, as the picture started to become clearer to him, "you kick up a bunch of shit, the Russians roll in with their tanks and kill maybe tens of thousands of their discontented satellite comrades.''

Kelly appeared amused for a moment, then his expression turned somber. "Something like that."

"So what?" Bolan growled. "You get a bunch of people slaughtered just to show the Russians you can play their game. Then everybody's back to square one."

"No, no, not at all. What we are hoping for is a major uprising in each and every ComBloc country. At the same time. With the bulk of the people behind the revolution. Out of any of Russia's satellites, East Germany has the best chance for victory and to break free of the Kremlin if this revolt can go off as the think tanks have proposed. So, if Russia has to send in hundreds of tanks, thousands of its soldiers into each of those countries, it will, in effect, neutralize its own military strength. Simply because the military machine will be broken up. The same thing happened to the Germans in World War II. They fought on one front too many, split, and ultimately neutralized themselves. Look, Bolan, the Afghans alone have managed to kick a few teeth out of the Kremlin. Just imagine what would happen if all of Russia's satellites wanted to go the distance with Moscow."

"The world would be pushed to the brink of war. It is insanity," Baknov suddenly said. "But what you say is true."

"Russia wouldn't risk a nuclear war, Bolan," Kelly quickly went on, "just to put down a few satellites.

The loss of some satellites would hurt them, to be sure, and they would lose a lot of face, but they'd let the Germans reunite.''

"You people hope, guy.''

Kelly shrugged. "We'll call their bluff, if we have to. Just like the Cuban missile crisis.''

"And risk incinerating half the globe?'' Bolan rasped.

Kelly rested a stony look on Bolan. "You got a better way?''

"Yeah,'' the Executioner growled. "Time. Keep fighting them, and hit them hard with their own fire. But time, guy, will ultimately dismantle the Soviet Union.''

"Or, *guy*,'' Kelly shot back, "time will ultimately dismantle NATO, and dismember the United States of America. Both sides are sitting on human time bombs. In both countries, there are major and seemingly unsolvable problems. And if those internal problems can't be solved, they will be crippling. They will bring death. End of ball game. End of country.

"Russia can't feed herself or her satellites. Here, the system is being vulturized by its own people. Here, the people who can do something to make things better are living in the now, taking all they can get. To hell with the future. Hell, there might not even be a future beyond the year 2000.''

"You're no prophet, soldier,'' Bolan said. "I don't think like you do. And I don't give a damn what the pretty boys in the think tanks say, or how many reports they throw around in the Senate and the Pentagon. They don't know. They are not out there. A computer doesn't replace experience. It doesn't make up for flesh and blood.''

"I wish I could be as optimistic as you, Mr. Bolan," Baknov said. "I have worked the British desk for the KGB for twelve years. NATO is weak, and it is on the verge of crumbling. Your CIA must do something to prevent all of Europe from falling to the Kremlin. Moscow would love nothing more than to have its tanks roll across Western Europe, and it is prepared to do so. The master list I compiled contained the names of key KGB agents inside NATO intelligence who could very well begin the downfall of Europe.

"But there is more to it than your CIA man has told," Baknov went on, grim. "Russia is preparing herself to make a major Middle East assault. Within the next three years. Once Afghanistan is completely conquered, Moscow will take Pakistan, and they could take Pakistan in the morning after breakfast."

"So, you see, Bolan," Kelly added, "it's not just Europe I was talking about. After Pakistan comes Iran, then Iraq. Russia is feeding both those countries arms so that when the Sunnis and the Shiites have completely kicked the shit out of each other, the Russian war machine can just roll right in and set up shop. And there won't be a goddamned thing we can do about it . . . short of pushing buttons."

"I have lived in Russia too long," Baknov said. "I am an old man. I have seen too much. I have seen too many die. It is a terror state. It is, as you Americans have called it, an evil empire. And perhaps Russia will somehow, someday be its own undoing. Like the Nazis." Baknov's voice choked with sudden emotion. "I had to desert...the Russian people are dying. The monster that is the Politburo, the dragon that is the KGB must be killed. Before it is too late...for everyone."

Bolan had nothing more to say to either Kelly or Baknov. There was no sense in arguing any point about any possible world conflict. Bolan wasn't much for debates, or discussion of politics. Talk was for those who couldn't or didn't have the means to act. He was a doer. He was a soldier. And if the situation was as desperate and as volatile as both men had just claimed, then he had to do something to close the wound both sides had opened.

Any damn way he could.

Even if that meant stepping between the CIA and the KGB in a cold war that had gone hot.

With his guns blazing. So both sides wanted to flex some muscle. That was fine with Bolan. He could do a little flexing, too.

And it would be best, he knew, if neither side came away with a thing.

Not the other's defectors.

And certainly not a clear-cut decisive victory in combat.

Before it was all over, Bolan knew there would be hell to pay.

The body count had just started.

Both sides were going for the throat.

And Mack Bolan was going to unleash his own special brand of hellfury.

As far as he was concerned it was winner take all. And at the moment it looked as if just as much harm could be done if the CIA came out on top.

Just what the hell had he walked into?

A death trap, yeah.

And its maw was widening by the moment.

Mack Bolan plowed on into the night. And discovered yet another wild card thrown into the deck at the LZ.

Jack Grimaldi had vanished.

But the Executioner knew who that wild card was. The Long Knives.

If longtime friend and war ally Grimaldi was harmed in any way, Bolan vowed to himself to settle that tab with the head of every last Long Knife redneck.

Kelly and Baknov stepped out of the truck as Bolan searched the cockpit and fuselage of the Bell.

"What is it?" Kelly asked.

Bolan checked his weapons crate. Mini-Uzi known as Little Lightning. Ten MK2 frag grenades. Weatherby Mark V .460 bolt-action rifle. Combat whitesuit for action on the Alaskan slopes. Spare clips for all hardware. Everything had been left untouched.

Bolan stepped through the fuselage door. "There's a right-wing fanatic gang called the Long Knives. You know them?"

Kelly nodded. "Yeah. I know of them, sure. They're on both ours and the FBI's list of terrorist groups to watch. Why?"

"They snatched my pilot."

"Maybe he's off in the woods taking a leak," Kelly suggested.

Bolan didn't even acknowledge that smart remark with a shake of his head. "Do you know if the Long Knives have a base?"

"Yeah, in fact, we reconned the perimeter of their compound before choosing a spot for the dummy safehouse. It's about ten klicks west. All back-mountain country. Are you going after your man?"

"I have to," the Executioner said curtly. "It's more than just losing a good pilot that would eat at my guts."

Bolan reached in through the fuselage doorway, grabbed the mini-Uzi and handed it and four spare 20-round clips to Kelly. "Think you can handle that?"

Kelly cocked Bolan a knowing grin. "I didn't just stumble out of Peary, pal. I can handle whatever you got in that bird."

Bolan chucked two MK2s to Kelly. "Then try these on for size."

"Christ, you must be expecting to go in and level that Long Knife base."

"If I have to," Bolan said, then strode toward the truck. "If I have to level their damn house to get my friend back in one piece, that's exactly what I'll do."

Kelly watched as Bolan hopped into the truck. He read the grim determination on the Executioner's face, recalled the hellzone the big renegade in blacksuit had created back at the saloon.

Special Operative James Kelly believed that Mack, the Bastard, Bolan was capable of doing anything he put his mind to.

Suddenly, the SOD man didn't feel so burdened.

Suddenly, he decided that fighting beside the Executioner would be his best bet against the KGB.

And that was still a long shot.

6

Milt Freeman didn't like what was happening to his country. Too many of the wrong people had the right say in the scheme of things. That meant everybody the left side of John Birch. And that meant something had to be done to save America before it was too late.

Yes, there was a disease spreading across the country. Freeman, who had often been told by an enemy of the American flag that he had a Napoleonic complex, called it a spiritual AIDS.

At five-two and 125 pounds it wasn't easy to miss Milt Freeman. That was, of course, only if he was lost in a crowd of kindergarteners.

But size had never deterred Freeman from imposing his will on others. People were seldom apt to disagree with a man who kept twenty submachine guns backing him up.

And machine guns were what the leader of the Long Knives specialized in.

Running drugs across the Mexico-U.S. border during the latter years of the Vietnam War had helped create the Long Knives and their gunrunning empire. Of course, back then Freeman had feverishly wished to go to Southeast Asia so he could, "bring a few gook ears back on his belt." But Uncle Sam had flatly rejected him. Yeah, a thumbs-down from the armed services because of his size. He would never forgive the Army for that. There was more than one G.I. or spit-and-polish officer on the Long Knives' target list.

Goddamn it, Freeman thought angrily. America, the land of the free, the home of the brave would get straightened out, or Milt Freeman wasn't going to stick around to see it perish because of Communist force and tyranny.

And a stint in the outlaw biker club, the Hellions, had shown him just how America could be straightened out. Better still, those days of riding in the wind had proved to him that a life in crime did, in fact, pay. Yeah, a broken head here, a busted kneecap there, a contract killing once in a while meant two things to Freeman. Money and power. They, in turn, secured respect.

The Long Knives had been around in the hills of West Virginia for the past six years. And Freeman was determined to see to their continued existence. As long as the cash flow from his black-market arms pipeline continued, and as long as the heads of the subverters kept rolling, the Long Knives would survive. Right now was a particularly prosperous time for the club. It seemed there were an awful lot of good ol' boys, Freeman thought, arming themselves these days with firepower that packed a rhino punch. Hell, Freeman could remember five years back when .38s and .22-caliber rifles had satisfied the demand for firepower.

Now the good ol' boys were buying everything in Magnum caliber, and the demand for assault rifles and SMGs had tripled in less than four months. Mostly, the Long Knives supplied every major outlaw motorcycle gang, the Ku Klux Klan, the Minutemen and weekend paramilitary-type warriors with firepower. But the market had boomed beyond just those principals. It had taken Freeman long years of hustling, and dozens of killings to get to his position as top dog.

Sure, it had been a tough road to get to the top. But it had all been worth the trouble. Law trouble. Biker trouble. He was smarter than the rest of the good ol' boys and the one-percenters. He knew how to get what he wanted. He knew how to use people. Like any good businessman, he had shrewdly used his "subordinates" to get to the top of the black market for U.S. arms.

Several of Freeman's gang members were vets. They had fought a war that he had been denied the privilege of fighting in. Resentment aside, he realized they had buddies still in the service who could provide access to a number of armories around the country. Of course, stealing weapons from Uncle Sam was a felony that carried with it a long prison sentence, Freeman knew. In his case breaking the law was a justifiable means to a common good end. His cause was the good of the people, the *real*, bona fide Americans. Since the flag-burning, pot-smoking, draft-card-burning sixties, when the American college campuses were full of yellow chickenshits screaming "Make Love, Not War," the country had become a dungheap of Commies, subverters, perverts and traitors. Freeman believed that someone now had to carry the Stars and Stripes into battle against the whores of freedom. Someone, in the name of what was right and just, had to wield the fire and the sword, and slay the dogs of immorality.

But how, Freeman wondered, could the Long Knives set an example for the rest of the country?

Hell, what the Long Knives desperately needed now was action. Hard-core, frontline action. Combat. Battle blood. Yeah, they needed a war, an excuse to flex their muscles and unleash some of the heavy firepower they'd stored up for the past few years. It wasn't enough that Freeman could send out a three-man execution squad to some small town or even an outlying suburb of a major city and assassinate left-wing chest-thumpers. No, he needed a hellzone where every last man of the thirty-five-member Long Knives could dig in, and test his fighting spirit to the limit.

The limit of death.

The limit of hell.

Milt Freeman believed that he might have just stumbled onto that war. And, if it was as big as he suspected, then the limits of death and hell were just what they would all be faced with.

Victory in that kind of war meant publicity for the Long Knives. Victory would widen his arms market, and that meant a massive cash flow. Victory would mark the road toward the return of America to its rightful owners.

Of course, Milt Freeman often wished he lived in South Africa. The Boers seemed to have all the right answers.

Freeman crouched over the bloodied, lumpy mask that was Jack Grimaldi's face. There was no emotion in the black marble eyes of the Long Knife leader as he looked down at the pilot.

A dozen Long Knives with AR-18s or Colt AR-15s encircled Freeman. An icy wind moaned through the barn, flickered the orange tongues of light in the kerosene lanterns.

"Okay, hero boy," Freeman began for the sixth time in the past hour since his men had stomped the stranger to a bloody pulp, "if you're not CIA, and you're not Special Forces or the Army's Delta Force, then who are you? And what's this business about a CIA war in Alaska?"

Grimaldi looked up at Freeman in defiant silence for a long moment. Air rasped through the pilot's split upper lip; blood spilled down the sides of his mouth.

Freeman chuckled softly, shook his head. He clasped his hands in his lap, looked around at the hard-eyed, shadowed faces of his troops.

"Listen, asshole," Freeman said, "if you don't start talkin', there ain't much I'm gonna be able to do to save your skin. I turn these here boys loose on your hide again, you're gonna be beggin' me to string you up. Now, why don't you be a good ol' boy, and tell me why you'd fly into our parts with a Huey."

"I already told you. I'm free-lance. And there's only one other guy."

Freeman found that amusing. Some of the other Long Knives did, too, and chuckled derisively.

"One man, sure, boy," Big Joe Lala growled. "One man's gonna go through six of our guys like he was raw cherries."

Freeman thought about that for a moment. What if the pilot was telling the truth? What if there was just the flyboy and one other man? Seven Long Knives slaughtered like sheep, Freeman thought. One man with his head chopped off his shoulders. And what was that all about anyway? Freeman didn't want to entertain the idea that it was just one man. Because if it was one man, then that son of a bitch was good. Damned good. A squad of commandos Freeman could deal with. But one good man who knew what he was doing, could make life very miserable for him and the Long Knives. Safety came in numbers, sure, Freeman believed, but that wouldn't stop a one-man hellsquad.

Something bothered Freeman greatly at that moment. He had a feeling that his captive was telling him the truth.

"Joe, Weebie," Freeman said, his black eyes like two obsidian chips in the murky light as he turned his head and looked at his men. "You get some of the boys around the perimeter. Double the guard. Shoot to kill anyone you see.''

"You believe the flyboy, Milt?" Weeb Jordan asked. "C'mon, I say we work him over some more."

Freeman shook his head. It was at a time like this that cooler heads had to prevail.

"No, no, man. Listen, he could end up being more useful to us alive than dead or half-dead. If it *is* one man, then that means these two are more than likely buddies. If there is just one other man, we either lure him in somehow, or kill him."

"Stands to reason, Milt," Lala said, "that something heavy's goin' down around here to bring those spooks from the CIA in. And what if these other dudes are CIA, too? Don't forget. It might've been our boys that snuffed them spooks."

"If it was, then that won't matter soon," Freeman replied. "Whoever his buddies are, they'll be coming in after this guy here. We can always pin those killings on them." Freeman stood, his gaze locked on Grimaldi. "Right, hero boy?"

Grimaldi said nothing.

Freeman smiled. "If it's war you people came out here lookin' for, then you came to the right place."

THE NIGHT ONCE AGAIN became an ally to Mack Bolan.

War was just what he intended to take to the Long Knives. The big nightscorcher had a nagging suspicion that the fanatic right-wing group was looking to cut itself in for a piece of the CIA-KGB action. Bolan decided to change their minds about that.

Permanently.

If the numbers permitted.

The Long Knives were a cancer that needed cutting out by the Bolan blitzkrieg, for damn sure. But at the moment, the soldier was more concerned about finding Jack Grimaldi in one piece and hauling his pilot friend safely away from the hardsite.

Damn the odds.

Damn this long night in hell.

There was no telling what the night would bring, Bolan knew, but he was ready to answer any grim reality. Armed with the silenced Baretta 93-R, garrote, Big Thunder and three MK2s, he was prepared to turn the Long Knife compound into a hillbilly dung heap if he had to.

Behind the shadow-warrior, CIA specialist James Kelly crouched under cover of some brush. Mini-Uzi in hand, the SOD man kept Baknov close by his side.

Bolan wasn't certain if he could trust the specialist to stand guard by the truck, sit tight. If all hell did break loose, Bolan knew the Company man would show his true colors under fire. Fight or bolt. The Executioner had given the guy that option.

Only because circumstance dictated the plan of action right then.

But Bolan knew the hearts of men, both good and bad. He read the agent as a warrior, primed and itching to get the fight under way against the KGB execution squads. Alaska was next on the Bolan hit list. Showdown on the last frontier, yeah. There, all hell would break loose with an apocalyptic roar. Bolan had no doubt about that. He sensed that Kelly, by opening up about clandestine Company operations in the heart of the East Bloc countries, felt he needed an ally after all.

Night vision goggles over his eyes, Bolan gave the hardsite a quick but thorough recon. The headshed was little more than a large farmhouse. There was a barn near what Bolan suspected was the paramilitary gang's headquarters. It was the aircraft beyond the barn that Bolan studied for a moment. Two twin-turbine choppers sat in a clearing beside a light twin-engine aircraft. These "patriots", he believed, had put together an efficient and deadly operation. Gunrunning, contract killing and, perhaps, drugs were the life blood of the Long Knives, Bolan decided.

Cannibals all the goddamned way.

The apparition in combat black swiftly moved down the wooded slope. He spotted activity near the barn as six assault-rifle-toting Long Knives stepped through the doorway. The distance to the barn was now more than a hundred yards, and the conversation that passed between the Knives escaped Bolan's ears.

But the crackle of a walkie-talkie didn't go unheard by the Executioner.

The guy was at the bottom of the slope, a mere shadow in the black gloom of night, but outlined clearly in Bolan's goggles.

Sentries.

Bolan opted for some intelligence first before a hard penetration. Holstering the Beretta, he fisted his garrote. The target was jabbering on in a low-pitched tone about seeing nothing unusual so far. As Bolan crept up behind the target, the guy also mentioned something about how he couldn't believe Freeman would think one man was responsible for the death of their "boys."

When he knew radio contact had been silenced, Bolan changed that line of thinking in a heartbeat.

Out of the night, the Executioner sprang like a panther on his target. Wrapping the garrote around the Long Knife's neck, Bolan dragged the guy back into the woods.

"Tell me what I want to know," the nightfighter snarled, twisting on the garrote, driving the Long Knife face first into the ground. "Or kiss West Virginia goodbye. I've got a friend somewhere here. Where is he?"

The Long Knife sputtered, gasping for air. "You s-son of a—"

"One second," the Executioner growled, tightened his deadly hold.

"In...the b-barn," the Long Knife managed to spit out.

"Numbers. How many there?"

"Th-three...you're history, boy. You'll be dead before you hit that barn door."

"Watch me," the Executioner rasped. "From hell," he added, and choked the life out of the Long Knife.

A shadow approached Bolan's position along the outer fringes of the woods.

"Hey, Junior," the shadow called.

Bolan upholstered his Beretta. Calmly, quickly he moved out from behind his cover.

The shadow froze.

Bolan didn't.

"Junior just went to visit ma and pa on the farm," the Executioner said, and punched the Long Knife a 9 mm eye on his forehead.

Two down, Bolan thought, but how many more? The only light on the compound shone from two windows in the farmhouse.

But he knew he would turn the darkness to his advantage. Obviously, the Long Knives were expecting company. They just hadn't guessed who was coming for dinner.

Death was the entrée.

The Executioner angled along the perimeter toward the barn, quickly cut the gap.

He dropped behind the cover of a tree for a moment. The barn was fifty yards directly ahead. If there were eyes in the hills, then he would have to chance it by moving across open ground to get to the barn. Soon enough, someone would discover the dead.

Strategy and careful planning had been the greatest allies to warrior Bolan throughout his hellstorming career. Recon was an invaluable tool to any soldier worth his stripes. Bolan never trusted chance, if there was a choice.

There was no such goddamn thing as the luck of the draw.

A fool relied on blind chance.

A savvy soldier always thought through his plan of action, from execution all the way to contingency in the event of disaster.

This night reeked of disaster.

Bolan couldn't shake the feeling of foreboding that crawled over his skin like leeches.

No thorough recon, no set plan here, he knew. Chance had taken an ugly turn.

It was get in and get out time. Any way he could.

He didn't like to operate that way, but there was very little he could damn well do about it at the moment.

Yeah, the wild cards kept stacking up.

Would fate now roll the black dice on him?

He took the discarded M-16 from the dead biker. Strategy.

Bolan holstered the Beretta. Then, holding the assault rifle at port arms, he moved away from the woods. With long, swift but careful strides he headed toward the barn. If there were watching eyes, and if he could look the part of one of them taking a stroll just long enough to get him to the barn and get him to Grimaldi, he'd worry about getting out after that.

Out of the corner of his eye, Bolan spotted a group of Long Knives moving away from the front steps of the farmhouse.

Twenty yards now to the target site.

A chill wind knifed through Bolan's blacksuit.

Someone was walking toward the killsite. Bolan bit down on a curse.

Ten yards ahead of Bolan the barn door creaked against the wind. He saw the flicker of light beyond the door.

"Hey, Junior, is that you, man?"

Damn!

The numbers dropped right into Bolan's lap. The group of Long Knives headed his way. He ignored them for another second. Then a shadow stepped through the barn doors.

"Hey!" the shadow in the doorway said, startled. "Who the hell—"

The Executioner answered the guy with a 3-round M-16 stammer to the chest.

Big Thunder snaked from leather.

Chance had just ripped this night asunder.

Bolan bolted the final few steps to the barn.

Let the numbers come, he thought.

The black dice were rolling.

7

Bolan stormed into the barn, Big Thunder booming instant death peals. Two targets, two dead men. The Long Knives standing guard over the outstretched figure of Grimaldi were hurled back, kicked off the barn wall by 240-grain hellriders as if they'd just slammed head-on into a freight train.

Grimaldi struggled to stand.

Bolan took one look at his friend's battered, blood-slicked features, felt an ice ball of fury lodge in the pit of his guts.

"Is it search and destroy time, Sarge?" the ace pilot cracked, wincing.

The guy was hanging on like the battle-hardened warrior the Executioner had always known and respected. He handed Grimaldi the M-16.

"You got it, buddy, from here on out. I hope you feel up to it."

"C'mon, big guy," Grimaldi said. "Count me in. Hell, they kicked me a few beauts, but I'm not exactly ready for the old folks' home."

Bolan checked the barn. If the Long Knives were any kind of soldiers at all, he knew they would try to surround the barn, seal off all doors and windows.

The Executioner pulled an MK2 from his webbing, handed it to Grimaldi, then took a frag grenade for himself. Someone was shouting orders outside, and Bolan heard the thud of boots over hard soil as the Long Knives encircled the barn. Damn right they had the action down, Bolan thought grimly.

"Take the stalls," Bolan told Grimaldi. "Let's hit them with the frags. Then break for the woods."

"Yeah, let's blow their stinking damn house down," the ace chopper pilot growled.

A window shattered beside Bolan and the snout of an AR-15 poked through the opening, but Bolan blew away the face behind that assault rifle with a quick double punch from Big Thunder.

"Now!" Bolan ordered Grimaldi, as he pulled the pin on his MK2.

Long Knives scrambled into position near the wide front entranceway as Bolan's frag bounced into the doorway.

Grimaldi lobbed his MK2, ducked behind a stall as autofire ripped into the wood above his head.

Long Knives filled the front and back doorways, muzzle-flashes winking. Hot lead geysered the dirt around Bolan as he dived for cover behind a stall. Cowboy hats and truckers' caps bobbed in the doorway behind the spitting muzzle flames, the Long Knives raking the barn floor with relentless autofire.

Then, one of the Long Knives spotted the frag bomb as it rolled beside him. His eyes widened in shock and horror, and he screamed, "Get the fuck—"

Too late.

Both frag grenades exploded simultaneously. Long Knives screamed in agony as shrapnel shredded their flesh. Dismembered, bloodied bodies were driven back into the night on crackling tongues of fire.

These good ol' boys should've stuck to their pick-ups and turkey shoots, Bolan thought, then bolted toward Grimaldi's position, scooping up an M-16. The pulverizing shock, both mental and physical, by the horrendous twin blasts had given the two warriors an edge, a vital few seconds to get the hell out of the scissoring field of fire.

Suddenly, Bolan stopped when he heard a familiar staccato burp, a long blistering Uzi spray that cut through the cries of pain, shouting and cursing around the clearing in front of the barn.

Crouched side by side, Bolan and Grimaldi looked toward the doorway. There, the heavy barn doors hung in strips from rotten hinges. Beyond the ruined doors, a secondary firefight raged on.

Through the swirling smoke Bolan and Grimaldi saw the black bulk of a truck racing toward the barn. The vehicle's lights were off, and it bore down on a group of Long Knives like a rampaging rhino.

If Bolan had any doubts about specialist James Kelly's heart before, they were now laid to rest. For the moment. Yeah, heroes sometimes had a way of becoming tarnished, Bolan knew. And the SOD man had proved nothing yet. It was hit or miss. For better or worse, the Company man was bought and paid for by the Executioner's war.

"The cavalry?" Grimaldi asked.

"Unexpected fire support," Bolan answered, tightlipped, watching with grim, wary eyes as the CIA agent plowed through the Long Knives, the sound of breaking bones loud through the air of battle as bodies cartwheeled over the hood of the truck like rag dolls.

A second later, the runaway assault truck bulldozed through the doorway. Wheels crunched over dead men as the side of the truck clipped the doorway. Giant pieces of wood flew across the barn. Long Knives swung into the doorway, assault rifles blazing.

But Bolan and Grimaldi didn't hesitate.

Kelly hit the headlights, swept the rig around. Recognition of Bolan showed on the specialist's grim face. And the Executioner didn't miss the streaks of blood on Kelly's face and neck as he and Grimaldi hopped into the pickup's bed.

Instantly, a blistering volley stung the side of the truck. Bolan and Grimaldi ducked for cover as the rig lurched away. Glass slivers from the punched-out back window littered the bed, bit into Bolan's arms and back. Shouting, cursing, filled his ears as more autofire ripped through the barn.

Kelly didn't have to be told the score. The Company man floored the gas pedal.

"Hold on!" he yelled through the window as the truck rocketed for the side of the barn, Baknov's head hammering off the back window frame.

Like some two-ton metal monster, the truck plowed through the stalls, shattering barn boards as it roared out into the open. Beams thudded off the roof and sides of the truck around Bolan and Grimaldi. Lead sizzlers whined off metal.

"Who is this crazy son of a bitch!" Grimaldi yelled over the hellfire din around them as Kelly jerked the rig hard to the left, surged across the open ground.

Bolan lunged up over the edge of the bed. Through his NVD goggles he made out the shadows scrambling around in the dust behind the speeding truck. Two rounds from the automag dropped a couple of pursuers. Grimaldi unleashed the M-16, stitched a trio of Long Knives through the sheet of black dust.

Within moments, the firefight was behind Bolan and Grimaldi.

The two men looked at each other.

"Damn, Striker," Grimaldi said, trying for a smile but grimacing instead. "And to think I was sipping mai tais in Waikiki a few days ago."

Bolan returned his friend's tight smile. "Stay hard, Jack. You're not ready for retirement yet. This one's just started to get hot."

"Yeah, hot, hell. Now we've got a bunch of good ol' boys straight from the heart of Dixie trying to get between us, the KGB and the CIA. Listen, there's more than one way to retire. One thing we'll never have to worry about, big guy. A pension plan.''

Grimaldi looked like hell. Bolan knew that as bad as his friend looked, he felt a damned sight worse because of the beating he'd suffered at the hands of the Long Knives. Even though there was a wry edge to his friend's voice, Bolan could let a little bitching slide at the moment. Jack had been pummeled, and Bolan couldn't be certain of the extent of the punishment until he had a chance to take a closer look at his friend. Letting off a little steam in the heated after-adrenaline rush of combat was good for some guys, Bolan knew.

Wearily, Grimaldi slumped back, hung his arms over the top of the bed. He heaved a sigh.

"How we doin' back there?" Kelly called, twisting his head around.

MILT FREEMAN HAD THE WAR he wanted. But as he surveyed the killzone he wasn't so sure he wanted that war after all. People were dying. And they belonged to him, dammit.

One lone son of a bitch had just walked straight into camp out of the goddamn hills and cut the fucking heart right out of them. That took balls. Freeman feared the grim reality of that. Yeah, he figured, maybe the Long Knives had bitten off a little more than they could chew. Hell, he raged to himself, whatever it was they'd bitten off they were now choking on!

"How many did they get?" he yelled at Weeb Jordan as Long Knives stormed around the compound, checking their dead, surveying the damage.

"I'm lookin' at maybe eleven, Snake," Jordan answered, striding angrily away from the barn.

"Maybe? Don't hand me any of that maybe shit, Weebie. Count 'em up."

Jordan said nothing, but the scowl that tugged at the sides of his bearded mouth darkened his simian features. "They'll be goin' back for that Huey, Snake. Let's get some boys on it, whaddya say?"

Freeman fought down his rage. He didn't like anybody, not even his second in command giving orders. There were times when Freeman thought Jordan was ready to push him around because of his size. But Jordan always gave ground. Yeah, Freeman thought, Weebie just wasn't that smart, and the *segundo* disliked and resented that. When it came to brains or muscle, brains usually won out. Freeman had long ago discovered Jordan had an inferiority complex about his lack of intelligence. And that was something Freeman always tried to exploit in others. Sure he was small, Freeman thought, but he could take charge, and when he gave orders people had better jump, or be looking for their balls somewhere down the road.

A little man had to dig deeper inside of himself than a big guy, he believed. It was the little guys who could be far more dangerous than any goddamn giant. Hell, history had been shaped by midgets. Napoleon. Stalin. Mussolini. Alexander the Great, who was also a queer. Hitler was a little too tall, but he was still smaller of stature than average. And that one lousy Austrian, a mongrel German, had shaped the ultimate destiny of mankind. World War II had been the dawn, the advent of the nuclear age.

Freeman had seen enough. The sight of the killzone, the very thought that his men had been cut down by one man knotted his guts with rage. He was going after those bastards. But now he had to seize control of the situation.

"Get those choppers loaded, Weebie," Freeman snapped. "Pack the fucking TNT. We're gonna nail those people. We'll follow their asses all the way to Alaska if we have to."

Several of the Long Knives looked at Freeman with dark concern, hesitated.

"Come on, goddammit! Get the lead out!" Snake Eyes rasped.

"You heard 'em," Jordan barked.

As the surviving Knives moved to comply with the order, Freeman surveyed the destruction once more. Who were these people? Just what the hell was going on? The pilot had mentioned Alaska. A war there between the Americans and the Russkis? Freeman cursed himself. He should've beaten more information out of the flyboy. Hell, Freeman thought, maybe he'd gone soft lately from lack of action. Nobody within three hundred square miles had ever tested the power of the

Long Knives before. Not even a roving pack of one-percenters.

Freeman felt the adrenaline burn through his blood. The war had come to him. Now, though, he had to take the war to this new and sudden enemy. Or lose face altogether with his troops.

This humiliation, he vowed to himself, would be avenged. Yeah, he would go to the ends of the earth to do it if he had to.

"How we gonna find them if they fly to Alaska, Snake?" Jordan wanted to know. "That ain't exactly—"

"We got radar, don't we," Freeman growled. "That's why we've got to get off the ground now! This is search and destroy, Weeb," he said, turning, looking Jordan dead in the eye. "Take no prisoners. Nobody left standing. You haven't lost your stomach for this, have you?"

Jordan looked offended. "Hell, no, man."

Freeman decided he'd better make sure the others felt that way, too. Fear was the best way to resecure his position as leader.

"You listen, Weebie. You tell all of our boys that their hearts better be in this. Anyone wants to pull out now, that's fine. But," he said, and paused for a heavy breath, "you make it a point to let them know that if they do that, they'd better be a thousand miles out of this county by the time we get back. I ain't takin' no losers. And we ain't gonna lose this thing, got me?"

Freeman looked at Jordan for a moment. He wasn't so certain his second in command understood.

Milt Freeman searched the dark look in Jordan's eyes.

He suddenly felt very small.

And very alone.

"HOW DO YOU FEEL, Jack?"

Grimaldi turned, looked at Bolan standing in the cockpit doorway. He gave the big guy the thumbs-up, then eased the Bell away from the LZ with a gentle increase of power.

"They didn't break anything, Striker. A few loose teeth, but I'm ready to roll. Next port of call. Cook Inlet, right?"

"You got it. Unless I hear otherwise from our Company man. I'm going to ask him a few questions now."

"We've got damn near a three-thousand-mile flight, guy. I've got all the fuel stops marked off en route to destination. But I don't know if I can give you an approximate ETA. It all depends on the weather, and ground delays. Well, you know how it goes."

"No sweat here, Jack. Just hold her steady," Bolan said, forced to speak loudly over the whine of rotor blades as the Bell climbed above the black hills of West Virginia. For a moment, he stared through the cockpit bubble at the blinking lights of Lee's Crossing in the distance. "It looks like our specialist may have just decided to play ball with us, after all."

"That's only because you're holding the ace in the hole, Striker. Where Baknov goes, there goes our specialist."

Bolan caught his friend wincing in pain. There were deep gashes on Grimaldi's face that needed stitching, and the purple lumps along his jaw had already swollen to golf-ball size. Bolan would like to settle the tab with the right-wing bastards, for damn sure. No, Grimaldi wouldn't have to twist his arm to get the green light to raze the Long Knives' compound with a Huey rocket burst.

But that was one tab that would have to wait.

Bolan was just glad that he'd gotten his friend out of there alive and whole. Yeah, he thought, it was more than just having a topnotch pilot at the helm. They had walked through more than one hellzone together. Grimaldi had a lot of guts. And he would always be right there, with his blood, if it came to that, to help win the war against the cannibals. And, in his war down the lonely hellfire trail, Mack Bolan knew it was damned good to have a guy like Grimaldi on his side. Grimaldi was one soldier who had earned his trust, respect and friendship a dozen or more times over.

Bolan left the cockpit and walked into the fuselage. There, Kelly and Baknov sat on a bench.

"Looks like I'm stuck with you, Bolan," Kelly said. "I just hope you know what you're doing."

As Kelly fired up a smoke, Bolan took a seat opposite the SOD man and the Russian.

"Don't hand me that line of crap, Kelly."

The specialist leveled a hard eye on the Man from Blood. "Come again?"

"I appreciate what you did back there. You helped us out of a tight spot."

Kelly shrugged, seemed skeptical. "Something any good soldier would've done."

"Just my point. As soon as we hit Alaska, I suspect your position's going to change."

Kelly was reading Bolan loud and clear.

And Kelly didn't like it.

He took a deep drag on his cigarette, poked a finger at Bolan.

"Hey, look, let's get something straight right here. My people are there at the zone now. Waiting. They want this piece of garbage," he growled, jerked his head sideways at Baknov. "And if I have anything to say about it, they'll get him. There's no question about my loyalty here. I'm not on your side, mister. I'm on our side. My side. That's it.

"This whole showdown's set to blow up in somebody's face, and I don't want to see any more of our guys wasted."

"Just what kind of people do you have there, Kelly?"

Kelly showed Bolan a twisted smile, let the smoke curl out of his nose. "My kind of people, buddy. Paramilitary operatives. A twenty-one-man killteam ready to storm that KGB safehouse. I got a man, my contact in Cook Inlet now, waiting word from me to move in. Colonel Thomas Blake. Ex-Special Forces. He's got some tough nuts under him. Couple of ex-Green Berets. Guys who quit Delta Force after that ungodly fuck-up, Desert One. Free-lancers. All of 'em have seen plenty of action. Nam. Afghanistan. Special operations in Central America.

"The bleeding hearts would call these guys gangsters, Bolan. Killers for hire. The kind of government employees who don't have to file income tax. They're a breed apart in the agency, and they'd just as soon kill something as look at it. Hell, even our own people refer to these guys as 'the animals.'"

Yeah, Bolan knew the type, all right. Not long ago he had crushed a gang of paramilitary operatives who'd gone renegade and set up a hellshop out in the New Mexico desert. Renegade specialists whose specialties had included murder for hire, terrorism, black-market arms and opium.

The paramilitary operative had a valid reason to operate in the espionage world, sure, Bolan believed. Uncle Sam had to use them as a force that could operate and act effectively outside of the guidelines of international law. When law wasn't respected, when animal man arrived in the picture, it took a very special kind of soldier to pick up the tab and meet the cannibal fire with fire.

The CIA had been playing second, even third fiddle to the KGB and Mossad for years. The press, the last administration had practically cut the balls off the CIA. What was the point in having a secret intelligence agency when nothing was secret anymore? In a world where unconventional warfare would shape the immediate future, the specialist, the clandestine counterterrorist strike forces, Bolan knew, would play a major role in fighting the current scourge of international terror-mongers.

As for the paramilitary operatives, they were indeed a rare breed, dedicated to subterfuge, mayhem and assassination, and their skills were beyond a doubt deadly and much needed in some war-torn arenas. The paramilitary operatives worked with and through the CIA, but they were independent contractors who were, in the end, answerable to no one. And like anything else, there were good PM operatives and bad ones—those who lived only for their own evil ambition, and spread the disease.

Suddenly, Kelly checked his chronometer. "In fact, I missed the check-in thirty minutes ago." He looked at Bolan. "Means something went wrong on this end. Means that execution squad will be moving out of Cook Inlet and heading north."

Bolan let the guy gloat for a moment.

"I'm assuming you know where the trade-off site is?"

"Of course," Kelly said, crooked a grin, dragged on his smoke. "I'll gladly show you people the way."

A thin smile appeared on Bolan's lips. "Get some shuteye," the Executioner said, his voice low-pitched, brittle with ice. "It's a long flight."

8

Ex-Special Forces Colonel Thomas Blake steered the black four-wheel-drive jeep up the winding, snow-covered road. He was three hours by gunship out of Cook Inlet. There, he had gotten word from his CIA contact. He had been informed that something had gone seriously, deadly wrong back at the dummy safehouse in West Virginia.

Company specialists had been discovered shot to death at the safehouse, and two CIA operatives had been slaughtered like cattle in a saloon in a nearby coal-mining town during a firefight with a KGB assassination squad.

The Soviet defector, Baknov, and Blake's operational contact back in the States were missing. According to first reports, gathered by intelligence through state and federal lawmen on the scene, there was a wild card now in the picture. A big, dark-haired, ice-eyed man in blacksuit with a cannon for a handgun. It was assumed by Intelligence that the wild card had both the Soviet defector and the Company man.

Reasons unknown.

Target unidentified.

But Blake now had his orders from the CIA. The orders he and his twenty-one-man hit squad had been waiting for all week deep in the heart of the Alaska Range.

They had been given the black light on Operation Bear Claw.

This was going to be a day, he vowed to himself, to remember. For once in his military career he was in charge from start to finish.

No, this wasn't Vietnam.

No, this wasn't the aborted disaster that had gone down in history as Desert One. That disaster in Iran boiled his blood every time he thought about it. A fuck-up, he knew from inside sources, that had happened in the Iranian desert because one too many officers had been bucking for promotion, and had to have their fingers in the goddamn pie. And because some guys, whom he would never care to mention by name, God damn them to hell, had lost their balls at the last minute.

But, this was his ball game. All the goddamn way. From planning, to the briefing of his troops, to the execution of the search and destroy mission.

America had been wearing a black eye since the fall of Saigon and the evacuation of her soldiers in disgrace in '75. The hostage crisis in Iran had blackened the other eye. Uncle Sam had become the court jester of the entire world, on both sides of the frigging Iron Curtain.

Special Operative Thomas Blake wasn't about to let his crack commando squad, which he'd code-named Strike Force Uncle Sam, get knocked out by the KGB.

Blake parked the jeep in front of the large cabin that housed his commando squad. The cabin sat on the rim of a plateau overlooking the sprawling, brawling ramshackle town of Taskinoma. Blake had done thorough research and reconnaissance on the town, because it was thirty kilometers southeast of "the zone."

Situated on the western fork of the Sustina River, the town had been abandoned by miners and prospectors after the Klondike Gold Rush at the turn of the century. Later, Blake knew, Taskinoma had been rediscovered, or rather, reshaped by an assortment of adventurers. Trappers. Pipeline workers. Loggers. Miners. Whalers. Prospectors. Bounty hunters tracking down fugitives. They came from all over the last frontier to sample this new Taskinoma. From the Yukon Flats, Kodiak, Juneau, Fairbanks, the Aleutian Islands. Even from British Columbia, and the far northern regions of the Brooks Range. Americans. Russians. Eskimos. A host of drifters, and a whole lot of trouble for any man who couldn't hold his own there. They came to Taskinoma to gamble, drink, whore and occasionally kill when the urge suited. The women, though, were the big item in the town. Sex for sale was the hottest commodity going in Taskinoma. Someone with the homing instincts of a vulture had long ago foreseen the woman problem. Human flesh had become the carrion to turn a bigger buck.

Because of the shortage of "available" women on the last frontier, prostitutes had been shipped from the States to Taskinoma. The women had been brought in by certain native flesh peddlers eager to fondle the abundance of crisp green Yankee dollars that flowed freely through the fingers of the hordes of men who worked on the eight-hundred-mile trans-Alaska oil pipeline. Wealth, Blake knew, often brought with it corruption. The colonel had forbidden any of his men to venture into Taskinoma.

The boys of Strike Force Uncle Sam were soldiers, he thought, not a bunch of goddamn playboys.

Blake stepped out of the jeep, grimaced against the blast of Arctic air. He pulled the hood of his parka up tight to his bearded, heavily lined features. Then he stood for a moment, gazing at the multihued bands of the aurora borealis shimmering to the north. The bright trails of light left by the stars glazed the black sky above the jagged, granite slopes. The dark winter sky swept by the northern lights—good sign or bad omen? Blake briefly wondered.

God, this is beautiful, haunting country, the colonel thought, pushing any pessimism aside.

This was a land alien to the rest of the earth.

This was one of the few remaining untamed wildernesses in the whole bloody world.

The land of the midnight sun.

This beautiful alien land, he knew, as he spotted the Huey UH-ID, the killteam's transport gunship, soaring over the northern outskirts of bawdy Taskinoma, was hours away from being besieged by hostile, invading forces.

With the break of dawn would come an outpouring of blood onto the snow.

Blake greeted ex-Army Captain Sam Benedict with a crisp salute as the man stepped through the cabin door.

"What's the word, Colonel?" Benedict wanted to know.

Blake glimpsed the tall, broad-shouldered Benedict. The man had done three tours of duty in Nam, had won enough metal and ribbons to decorate a Christmas tree. Body counts had been Benedict's specialty. A walk in the sun with Benedict had usually meant a walk into hell for NVA regulars. Benedict had a nose for enemy blood like a hound dog. The man was soldier, assassin, tactician all wound up into one fighting machine set on autodestruction. Search and destroy. Scorched earth. And damn anybody on the other side who got in the way. Blake liked the guy, and had made Benedict his second in charge of Operation Bear Claw.

"We've got ourselves a black light operation on this one, Captain," Blake said, and brushed past Benedict, stepping into the warm confines of the cabin. "All systems go. Search and destroy."

The commandos of Strike Force Uncle Sam turned immediate attention on Blake. There was a grim tension in the room that Blake instantly sensed, and liked.

These soldiers were ready to go, he thought. Soldiers itching to kick a little butt. By God, they were going to get their chance to burn some Red ass!

Blake strode across the wood floor toward the pot-bellied, cast-iron stove. He poured himself a cup of coffee. Then he turned to address his troops. All of them were dressed in combat whitesuit, their webbing fitted with frag grenades, their M-16s with attached M-203 grenade launchers by their sides. The LAWs, Blake knew, would be handed out when the gunship hit the slopes near Mount McKinley.

Blake took a long moment to search the faces of his troops. They were lean, hard, tough men. This was war, and they all knew it. All of them had seen action in plenty of hotspots, in numerous clandestine wars around the world. Hard-bitten and cynical, because they'd had the short end of the stick rammed up their asses in Nam. And later, for some of them, with Delta Force during Desert One. There was only one way to fight, Blake knew.

Fight to win, get the hell out and move on to the next LZ. War was what man really wanted. Peace was bullshit. Man was basically an animal, a predator. And warrior man needed to exercise those primal urges to hunt, to fight, to conquer.

Blake figured that before long America would be fully involved in the Central American conflict. But in a way he dreaded that day.

And for a damned good reason.

Too many sons of bitches still hadn't learned their lesson from Nam. Congress was even now haggling over the amount of money to send, and when to send it, to the contra rebels in Nicaragua, but with some justification, Blake thought. The Central America question could be solved inside a month. *If* only the armed forces were allowed to fight total war. On their own terms.

Total war on his terms was what he and his strike force were about to initiate.

"All right, you men," Blake began. "We go out of here at 0730. We've been given the black light from upstairs. Get Snipes and Dover at any cost. Terminate all targets, principal and secondary."

"Now, you've seen the aerial recon photos of that mountain range. The safehouse is situated at the top of a trail on the east side of the range, in full view from the bottom of the main trail. I'd say that the KGB is expecting us. And inviting us. They've already hit the CIA back in the States. Yeah, the goddamned bastards have won the opening round."

This drew no reaction from any of Blake's commandos. Good, the colonel thought, they were as cold as ice. No fear. No anger. No visible sign of vengeance.

"You have been divided up into seven three-man fireteams," Blake said. He sipped at his coffee. "There will be one team on the snowmobiles for emergency contingency action and resupply. I expect we'll get a good fight from the Russians, but I don't expect them to hold up. They are fighting on our turf, so they couldn't exactly bring a battalion across the Bering Strait.

"However, if worse comes to worst, and it looks like we can't get at Snipes and Dover, we hit the target area with the LAWs. If we can't get those two bastards back, then we sure as hell aren't going to leave the Russkis with them, either.

"The Soviet defector has been declared missing, presumably kidnapped by an unidentified wild card. So keep your eyes peeled and ears open for any unexpected visitors. I want very few surprises on this. We've been told to pull out all the stops on the operation."

Blake was about to mention the "grave consequences of failure," but caught himself in time. A fighter, a warrior, never thought about losing, or about the humiliating consequences that came with failure. A warrior thought only about winning. A warrior saw only the enemy crushed. When a man started to dwell on losing, on the "what ifs," he generally lost. And when Blake thought about that, he thought about Vietnam.

There was something else that bothered Blake. His initial air recon of the zone had reported a KGB surveillance of a U.S. government research facility for the criminally insane. Jarkin Institute was nine kilometers north of the target site, in what Blake referred to as the DMZ. But the Soviets, he knew, would recognize no demilitarized zone in this head-on conflict; there would be no rules in this dirty, clandestine battle. Why the KGB had a team near the institute puzzled the colonel. Jarkin was a maximum-security asylum. And Blake suspected that the Soviets had more than just a passing curiosity about the institute.

Still, reconnaissance teams could not put a finger on what it was the KGB was up to with their surveillance of the asylum. He had pressed his recon team about this, but they had finally agreed that the Soviets were merely doing some reconnaissance of their own. For some reason, Blake didn't believe that. But without any concrete evidence of some sabotage against the institute, the colonel was forced to put the issue out of his mind.

"Okay," Blake finished, "final weapons and gear inspection. Let's buckle up, and knuckle down. The gunship's on its way now. Any questions?"

Dark eyes set in the hollow rings of bearded faces stared back at Blake.

There were no questions.

Colonel Blake heard only the soughing of the wind outside the cabin.

SERGEY KOVEKNY WAS DISGUSTED.

Disgusted to the point of murder.

The American spies had long outlived their usefulness. But he had to keep them alive.

They were now the bait he needed to lure in the CIA assassins.

Perhaps, he decided, they would serve far greater usefulness in death. They had most certainly done little for him in life.

Even though he had hacked off the fingers on both hands of the two imperialist spies with a meat cleaver, and even though he had scalded every inch of their bodies with boiling water, Kovekny still racked his brain in search of other ways he could torture the American traitors.

For the time being, he contented himself with lashing the pulped, blood-slickened masks of Snipes and Dover with the back of his leather-gloved hand. The crack of leather off flesh sounded like a pistol crack in the small, empty confines of the cabin.

Empty, except for the wooden boxes Kovekny's men had piled along the walls. Those boxes, the KGB assassin knew, contained the final utilities that would serve Snipes and Dover the justice they so much deserved for betraying their country.

Kovekny had given up hours ago on luring the CIA gangsters up the trail with the screams of agony he had forced from the mouths of the Americans. *Nyet*, they could not withstand a little punishment. They would have lasted all of six weeks in a Siberian concentration camp. They were weak and soft, and Kovekny could feel only a deep loathing for them. Like old women, the two Americans kept fainting under torture. Now, Kovekny could do little more than spark a glimmer of defiant hatred in their eyes with his hand-lashing. With each vicious blow, he jolted their heads from side to side, cursed them. Strapped to thick wooden chairs that resembled those used for electrocution, Kovekny's prisoners could do nothing but ride out the torture.

And bleed.

And frequently pass out.

Finally Kovekny grew tired of the torture, sickened by his inability to produce even a whimper of pain from the lips of the two men.

Kovekny drew himself erect. He recalled the endless hours of interrogation he had put the two defectors through back at KGB headquarters, Moscow. Beatings. Drugs. Threats against their families. Kovekny recalled how he had played the role of the "bad guy," while the thickset, black-haired agent now standing next to him had played the role of the "good guy."

Kovekny looked at Boris Stevhkin. "Look at them. They are idiots. Self-serving. Decadent. For mere money they would sell out their own country. Like a piece of merchandise, they are bought and sold so easily. The very sight of them disgusts me!"

Kovekny looked at the glassy stare that found him through the lumpy, black-and-purple folds around Dover's eyes. "I hope you heard that, indeed. Your life belongs to me. Your CIA comes now to try and rescue you. They will be removing garbage off our hands. They will fail. You will all die.''

''Do you not think I know what it is you are both doing? Did you think me so stupid as to believe you were just buying yourselves time with this ridiculous lie you came to me with, about Star Wars? For twenty thousand of your dollars you threw away your lives. I knew from the minute I looked at those documents and that microfilm, that they were phony. Fools! Your government announces to the world their SDI. As if this will bring our premier to his knees. As if your country can now make demands on Russia to disarm.''

Dover drew his lips back over crimson-stained teeth.

Kovekny waited for the man to say something, but he only groaned in pain.

''Comrade Kovekny,'' Stevhkin said, his hands folded behind his back. ''Comrade Kosygin awaits your orders. Word from Colonel Belokai is that the great traitor has been taken by a third party. The colonel claimed the third party was the Executioner.''

''I know, comrade,'' Kovekny replied. He wished that Stevhkin would stop mentioning that name, the force that had penetrated the heart of Moscow and wreaked havoc on the KGB and its operations around the world. If it was this Mack Bolan he had heard so much about, then he wanted to be certain before he alerted any of his other agents. That name alone, the Executioner, seemed to instill instant fear in the hearts of KGB operatives. It made Kovekny sick that one man could create such fear, even in absence.

Still, he knew the untainted, brilliant record of Colonel Belokai, hero in the Great Patriotic War against the Nazis. And still he knew what kind of man Belokai was. He had suspected all along that Belokai was a man given to the pursuit of heroic deeds at the expense of overall KGB operations. Perhaps now, Kovekny hoped, the colonel would show his true character, if, indeed, this Executioner was looking to test the strength of the KGB once again. Perhaps now the colonel would prove that his own suspicions were founded in truth. Comrade Belokai had been looked upon by Moscow as a noble fighter for too long. It was time someone showed the Kremlin that Belokai was not as tall as he stood.

"Your orders, Comrade Kovekny."

"My orders are this, tovarich," Kovekny said somberly. "You will radio Comrade Kosygin. He is to proceed immediately with the attack against the asylum. He is to kill all guards, all personnel. He is then to free and arm every last inmate. Any inmate who he feels will be uncooperative in this matter he will execute on the spot. I have been informed that the CIA killteam has assembled in Taskinoma. Their helicopter gunship has been sighted, and we must assume that they know what took place at the CIA's safehouse in their state called West Virginia. Therefore, we must prepare for them to begin their attack. As soon as they are spotted near our perimeter we will begin our attack.''

"I want the way made clear to this cabin, so clear, in fact, tovarich, that the CIA gangsters will be able to proceed virtually unmolested up the trail.''

"Also, alert our firebase, and tell them they are under orders to blow any aircraft out of the sky. Any aircraft. Civilian, military or otherwise. Failure to do so will mean the severest of penalties. I cannot wait for the colonel's return. Do you understand?''

"Perfectly, Comrade Kovekny. And what of this Executioner? What if he had Baknov? Moscow would surely want us to eliminate the Executioner for good, is that not so?''

Kovekny tried to keep the impatience out of his voice. Stevhkin was questioning his orders, and that meant the man was also questioning his leadership.

"We will deal with that matter as soon as it presents itself. If it is true that the Executioner has shown himself in this, then I tell you,'' Kovekny said, turning and looking Stevhkin dead in the eye, "he will not live to see the midnight sun.''

The two KGB killers looked at each other for a long moment.

Finally Stevhkin nodded. "I hope not, Comrade Kovekny. It was made quite clear to us before leaving Moscow what would happen if we failed in our struggle against the CIA gangsters. It would be far worse,'' he added, "if our agents failed against the Executioner...again.''

Kovekny looked away from Stevhkin. He knew the consequences of failure would be disastrous.

''Go,'' he told Stevhkin.

Stevhkin had just reminded him of a possibility he dreaded far worse than anything else.

Failure.

That meant death.

As certain as death awaited the great traitor, Baknov.

As certain as death awaited any man who was not prepared to win this war.

9

The best attack was most often the direct, or shock, attack.

Anastas Kosygin had learned that nine years ago at a Committee training base in Vortuka. Later, that piece of tactical philosophy hadn't served him, nor the Russian army so well in their war to liberate Afghanistan.

During a briefing at KGB headquarters over the Afghanistan invasion, Kosygin recalled that one officer had remarked how beautifully shock attacks had worked for the Germans. The insinuation by that officer had been clear to KGB General Alexey Zomatov back then. The Germans were a smarter race, and therefore the Nazis, with their superior intelligence and ruthless disciplines, had been better equipped for military strategy and conquest. That particular officer, Kosygin remembered, had then been shot in the face at point-blank range by General Zomotov.

The truth had clearly enraged the general. One killing shot in that room had undoubtedly changed the atmosphere of the briefing. It was a tactic the Great One, Stalin, often employed. Kill one, get the attention of many. Except that the Great One had killed many, and clearly gotten the attention of all.

Still—and this had left a bitter taste in the mouth of the Kremlin—the failed Russian "shock invasion" against Kabul had only begun a war that, Kosygin knew, would drag on for decades. After that gamble and the initial failure of the December '79 invasion, Moscow tried a different tactic. A lingering conflict with Afghan tribal warriors did not appeal to the Kremlin, but there seemed to be little they could do about it, short of nuking the countryside. But total annihilation was not the objective of Soviet expansion, nor was scorched earth the point of Soviet conquest. So the new tactics employed in Afghanistan were patience, propaganda and, of course, constant brutality against the Afghan Islamic guerrillas, the mujahedeen.

Employ antiterrorist tactics. Chemical warfare. Constant, relentless artillery shelling and MiG strafing. Mine and booby-trap the countryside. Raze every village by fire and blood, and scatter the villagers to the wind. No matter what it took to conquer Afghanistan, Kosygin knew that the Afghans couldn't hold strong against the massive military might of the motherland.

The Afghans would crumble, then Pakistan would fall next, he knew.

Anastas Kosygin had so far played a heavy hand in undermining the government of Kabul. Under his skilled direction, the KGB had inserted Communist bureaucrats into every Afghan city. Now it was the KGB who pulled the strings within the Afghan government.

Kosygin had personally trained the members of KHAD, the Afghan secret police, and KHAD was now the effective Afghan arm of the KGB. Lesson number two he had learned at Vortuka: an indirect attack, from within the enemy's ranks, was sometimes more effective than a direct attack. Dissension from within the ranks often meant that group's suicide. Another country's dissension, people's malice toward their own government, were the KGB's greatest weapons. There were many subtle ways to defeat an enemy besides outright attack, Kosygin had been taught.

At the moment Anastas Kosygin had no options. He had his orders from Kovekny. Attack Jarkin. Swift, direct assault, and take no prisoners. He would do precisely as he was ordered. He would succeed without question. He would not be left holding the wrong edge of the blade in this war against the CIA.

From the snow-covered timber slopes surrounding the low-level, white-walled compound, Kosygin gave the rocket teams the signal by radio. Then he radioed the transport truck, ordered the driver to move in.

Kosygin watched as the severed ends of electrical lines crackled to the east, the sparking, entwined lines falling to the snow. An emergency generator immediately powered the institute. Light bathed the rooms behind the iron-barred windows of Jarkin. Floodlights burned to life, swept a glaring white light over the grounds behind the low concrete wall.

The guard in the tower flicked on his spotlight, began raking the slopes with his beam.

A second later, Kosygin saw the trio of flaming, smoking lines streak toward the institute, the RPG-7 missiles zeroing in on targets. The watchtower and the huge radar dish in the courtyard were evaporated by roiling fireballs. The third projectile blew in the front gate.

Fifteen KGB agents stormed the walls from all points east, west, north and south.

Kosygin checked his watch, then snatched up his AK-47.

The transport truck rumbled down the trail behind Kosygin. As the truck stopped, the KGB assassin flung open the door, hopped into the cab. In the distance, the staccato din of RPK-74 and AK-47 fire ripped apart the early-morning air.

Kosygin felt his pulse pounding in his temples as the driver left the trail, roared toward the devastated gateway. The sound of war invigorated him.

"Hurry!" Kosygin rasped.

As the vehicle surged across the compound a siren began to wail. Kosygin saw two of his men blast the siren box from its mount with a quick burst.

Agents crashed through the front double doors.

Kosygin jumped out of the truck, ran to join his comrades.

Screams of terror sounded beyond the doors.

Autofire silenced pleas for mercy.

The sound of death excited Kosygin. He took the six steps to the foyer two at a time.

Half of his assault force, he knew, had stormed the facility from the back. The attack had happened lightning fast, and Kosygin was pleased. They had succeeded.

As he rounded the corner of the front entrance, Kosygin looked both ways along the hall. The walls were red with blood. A half-dozen guards were strewed up and down the hallway; discarded M-16s lay on the floor near lifeless, twitching hands.

Kosygin raced down the corridor, shouting orders. "Round up all administrative personnel! Find the inmates and assemble them in the foyer!"

Kosygin glanced at his watch. Thirty-five seconds from the initial RPG rocket-fire to the takeover. He was greatly pleased. He hoped Kovekny would remember this in his report to General Zomatov.

Kosygin found the radio room. There was an orderly working the console in a furious attempt to raise help. The orderly looked at Kosygin in horror, started to scream a plea as the assault rifle swung his way. The killer shredded the man with 7.62 mm lead.

Then Kosygin hosed the radio console with a fusillade.

Returning his attention to the hallway, the Russian heard the terrified cries of women, the screams of the dying as his men executed prisoners.

At the far end of the hallway, Kosygin saw his men ushering inmates from the ward. A part of Kosygin told him that it was insane to do this. But a good soldier never questioned his orders from a superior. The inmates were to be armed and turned loose.

And the inmates would be drugged by Metaclyn, he knew. Metaclyn was a potent mixture of amphetamine and human adrenaline laced with a rare and volatile hallucinogen, pallicuxx, which was grown in Southeast Asia. The KGB had recently experimented with Metaclyn on enemies of the state. The effects were horrifying. Metaclyn turned the subject into a raving lunatic, a mindless monster who would kill anything and everything in sight. The KGB was prepared to administer the drug in widespread doses to captured rebels in Afghanistan, and turn them loose on their own people. It was part of ''newer'' tactics Moscow was ready to employ. War was costly, and the foray into Afghanistan was costing Russia plenty.

Kosygin was grimly aware, as he looked at the hollow-eyed, gaunt faces of the assembled inmates in the foyer, that he already had a pack of madmen, schizoids, psychotics and psychopaths on his hands. They were all dangerous, mindless animals, even without a dose of Metaclyn. That was good, he thought. It would all work to his advantage. Given to the lunatics, the Metaclyn would ensure the KGB's success in their Alaskan war against the CIA.

There would be no failure, he told himself. His life depended on it.

Kosygin waited until all eighty-five inmates were brought to him in the foyer. There, too, the surviving doctors, nurses and orderlies were gathered. Kosygin instructed his men to line the hospital staff up against the wall.

As the assassin searched the faces of the inmates he thought for a moment that he was looking at Death. Walking, living death was staring back at him. Graveyard shells of men and women. Every last one of them hopelessly, criminally insane. He felt their haunted, fixed gazes crawling over his flesh. It was unnerving. The sooner this business was over, the sooner he set the inmates free, the better, he thought.

One of the inmates suddenly became hysterical, began shouting, "No! I won't let you! I won't let you kill me!"

Kosygin turned at the hip, drove the hysterical inmate back into the wall with a 3-round stammer from his Kalashnikov.

Excellent, the KGB killer thought, as he felt the shocked silence wash over him. Kill one, get the attention of all.

It worked.

"Wh-who are you people?" a short, wiry, bald-headed man with thick glasses asked Kosygin.

Kosygin read the doctor's nameplate on his smock. Bronkowski. Good, he thought, a Pole. Kosygin wanted to make an example of this Pole, but within moments, he knew, they would all be examples.

"Comrade Bronkowski," Kosygin began, his voice steady, low-pitched. "Understand that I will ask the questions here. First, are you in charge?"

Bronkowski gave Kosygin a jerky nod. "Y-yes... I am. My God, man, this is a research facility. You have no right—"

"Silence!" Kosygin snarled. "This is a prison," he barked, turning his attention toward the inmates as his men trained their weapons on the hostaged group. "This... place is a deathhouse. Do you people understand this?"

The lunatics just stared back at Kosygin with glassy, empty eyes.

"What is the matter with them?" Kosygin growled at Bronkowski.

"They are drugged. Sedated. That's the only way we can work with them."

"Work with them?"

"Yes," Bronkowski faltered. "Brain scans. Autosomal dominance research."

"Genetic experimentation?" Kosygin pushed.

"Y-yes, well, sort of... It's all legitimate. It's all funded by—"

"Do you people hear that?" Kosygin said to the inmates, knowing full well that they understood very little of what he said. "How many of you know what a frontal lobotomy is?"

"I do," a tall, broad-shouldered inmate with long, scraggly brown hair said.

Kosygin carefully looked at the man. He had found a live one. He must choose his next words carefully, he decided. He must keep them all off guard, frightened.

"We have come to free you from this institution," Kosygin said. "Which, I may add, is nothing more than a prison. This place is meant to keep you under its domination until your guards—all of whom have lied to you that they are your doctors, that they are interested in your health and well-being—see fit to use you as live experiments."

Bronkowski began to tremble. His face turned ashen.

"They mean to cut into your brains," Kosygin said, saw horror creep across the faces of several inmates, read the rage that began to simmer in the eyes of other lunatics. "They mean to see how you will respond to electric shock placed on certain areas of your brain. In effect, comrades, they mean to kill you eventually. But only after you have suffered terribly. We, comrades, are here to free you from your tormentors. We are your friends who have come to save your lives. Before all of you are killed by these imposters," Kosygin said, turning, holding out a hand toward the hostage hospital staff.

Bronkowski's head shook violently, caused the glasses to slide off his nose, fall and shatter on the floor. "Liar. Liar!" he screamed.

Kosygin gestured to his men, nodding at the hospital staff.

A dozen AK-47s opened up. A hurricane of ComBloc lead chewed up the captured hospital staff. Screams were instantly cut off as the assassins raked the bodies with autofire, blood splattering the white wall, arms and legs flailing in death throes.

None of the inmates moved. They just stared at the toppling, bullet-ravaged corpses with wide-eyed, impassive expressions.

When the last of the dead hit the floor, Kosygin ordered his men, "Quickly. Move these people outside."

Kosygin stepped out into the cold morning air. To the east the first rays of sunlight penetrated the mist that shrouded the mountains. Patches of thick gray cloud cover hung over the compound. Kosygin glanced at the sky as his men ushered the inmates toward the transport truck. Suddenly, Anastas Kosygin felt old. Very old and tired. And he didn't understand why.

He should have been used to the grim weather, the brutal cold and the knifing winds. But for some reason the older he got, the longer he worked for the KGB, the harder it became to endure harsh weather. He would never dare tell any of his comrades this. They would think he had lost his mind. Or had developed misplaced loyalties.

Quickly, the agents under Kosygin's supervision pulled an array of weapons from the transport truck. They handed AK-47s, Makarov autopistols and RPK-74s to twenty of the lunatics.

"What is this?"

Kosygin turned, looked at the man who had voiced the question. It was the tall, brown-haired inmate. Kosygin smiled at the man. He had leadership potential, Kosygin decided. There was cunning, discernment in the inmate's eyes. The others would surely rally around this man.

"This, comrade," Kosygin said, "is your path to freedom. There are men, right now, coming to kill you. They come from the woods, and they come heavily armed. These men I speak of, they come from the town of Taskinoma. Do you know which town I speak of?"

The man nodded.

"Good. Then, I suggest you march there as quickly as possible and kill those people. Before they kill you," Kosygin said in a loud voice, addressing the entire mob.

"But . . . we'll freeze," the tall inmate said.

Kosygin looked at the man. There was a sudden dangerous glint in his eyes. Kosygin noticed that many of the inmates were already shivering. He waited until the rest of the weapons had been distributed. It was always best to make children wait. And he was dealing with children. Very dangerous children.

To ensure that their assault on the town was not a one-sided slaughter, Kosygin's men handed out hatchets, pitchforks, butcher knives, hammers and garrotes to the rest of the inmates. Kosygin knew that the townsmen would fight back. Kovekny had already briefed him on this. It was hoped that the lunatics would run into the CIA fireteams. Perhaps the sudden horror of being faced down by a pack of bloodthirsty, insane killers would soften up the CIA. Perhaps the CIA would then flee the horror. Perhaps the lunatics would take care of the CIA gangsters for the KGB. Or, at the least, the CIA would retreat to Taskinoma and attempt to save the townspeople from the murdering clutches of the lunatic mob.

That had been Kovekny's reasoning. And Kosygin had agreed with Comrade Kovekny.

"Yes, of course." Kosygin smiled at the shivering mob. "You are cold, comrades. We will take care of you."

Kosygin nodded at the agents standing in the bed of the truck. Those agents dumped heavy fur coats and hats on the ground.

Because they were sedated, the lunatics moved slowly toward the furs.

And, because they were drugged, Kosygin knew their minds, even in a deranged state, had not yet registered what was happening at the moment.

The Metaclyn would take care of that.

The Metaclyn was passed out after the coats and hats were distributed.

Kosygin watched as the thermos containers moved from hand to hand. The liquid they drank had been warmed, then sweetened by a powdery substance. What they drank, Kosygin knew, tasted something like cider.

But within fifteen minutes there would be a fire raging inside each lunatic that they would not be able to put out.

"Drink up, comrades," Kosygin encouraged. "It is a long walk to the town and you must have energy. You must be warm. You must be ready."

Kosygin turned away from the mob, signaled for his men that it was time to get out of there.

The dead, the KGB assassin knew, were rising from the grave.

Kosygin did not want to be there when that happened.

He wanted to put that place behind him.

It was a frightening ploy, he thought, to use lunatics, the dead, like this, to assure victory. He only hoped this decision would not come back to haunt them all.

He glanced up at the gray sky before climbing into the cab of the transport truck. An oppressive weight seemed to drop square down on his shoulders as an icy wind sliced through his parka.

The sky looked like the lid of a coffin, he thought.

10

Colonel Thomas Blake was seething. But he simmered in hard silence.

Operation Bear Claw was off to a bad start, and the strike force had not even disembarked from the gunship to the mission's LZ yet.

He checked his watch. 1055. Christ! Damn near three and a half hours behind schedule.

A pretakeoff check of the Huey by the pilot had discovered some serious malfunctions. Something about the directional control pedals, or rudders in civilian talk. Something about failure of the rotor hub. Blake didn't care to know the details, he just told the guy to get on it and get the goddamn lead out. Hell, almost every man in the strike force had flown in slicks on dozens of missions in Nam. They didn't need a lecture on the instability of the helicopter.

Next time out, Blake decided, he'd handpick his own flight crew. He was sick and tired of the fucking suits back at Langley calling all the shots. What the hell did they know, anyway? It wasn't their ass out there getting shot at.

He knew one thing. If the Huey failed now, he'd have that pilot's head. Any possible equipment failure should have been checked out twenty-four hours ago. He'd make sure the pilot never flew again. Had to be a Marine pilot, Blake thought. The kind that had lost their balls over in I-ran. Blake liked seeing some son of a bitch squirm when he started chewing ass.

First off, Blake hated like hell to make a drop-off in the middle of the day. That kind of LZ had a way of turning hot in a hurry. If they landed under fire, he'd be chewing one hotshot pilot's ass all the way back to the Pentagon.

There was just no goddamn excuse for this kind of delay.

The intercom above Blake's head crackled with the pilot's voice.

"One minute to the landing zone, Colonel. Looks clear from where I sit."

Looks clear from where he sits, Blake heard his mind growl. Christ, the guy would probably drink out of Lake Erie, too.

Colonel Blake looked at his assembled twenty-one-man killteam. Dressed in combat whitesuit, each man carried an M-16A2 with grenade launcher. Webbing included four frag grenades, five 30-round clips of 7.62 NATO slugs, garrote and commando knife.

Dressed and ready to kill.

Blake checked his assault rifle, made sure a round was chambered. He stood, said, "Hit the LZ and move out. I want as little radio contact as possible, just in case they're tapping in on our frequency. If that's the case, we use diversionary movement. Either way, you move in, move up. But always move ahead."

Blake nodded at Captain Benedict, who threw back the fuselage door.

Blake checked the terrain. Snow-covered timber slopes ringed the LZ. Granite peaks towered to the north and to the east. This was wild, rugged country. Lakes, gorges, and who knows what else, he thought.

For a moment, the colonel peered at the thick mist that cloaked the slopes to the north, south and east. The KGB hole-up was ten klicks due north. The mist presented unseen enemy positions. This was American territory, but it was anybody's domain.

The death hunt would see to that.

The gunship's skids touched down in snow.

"Good luck, Colonel," the pilot said over the intercom.

Blake couldn't resist. He pushed the intercom button. "Luck's for assholes, boy. You just make sure you meet those rendezvous times. Read me?"

"Roger that, Colonel. Listen, I'm sorry about that delay, but hey, what the hell was I supposed to do?"

"Stop your whining, mister," Blake growled. "If you'd done your job and checked this bird yesterday like you should have, you wouldn't be sniveling all over yourself now like some schoolgirl."

Blake punched off the intercom in disgust. He and Benedict hopped out of the fuselage, the rotor wash whipping snow up at their faces. Quickly, the colonel and the captain led their three-man fireteams into the woods.

A metal ramp hit the LZ. Soldiers guided the two snowmobiles down the ramp. An M-60 machine gun was mounted on each snowmobile.

Blake crouched behind a tree, peered up the slope. It would be a tough hike to the KGB hideout. Foot by foot. Klick by klick. Bad light, and unfamiliar turf.

It was dark at the top of the slope. There, Blake looked for signs of life, any dancing shadow. He found nothing.

The colonel signaled Benedict.

The captain's fireteam moved out.

The snowmobiles fired to life.

The gunship lifted off.

Blake turned, watched the other three units advance toward his position. The snowmobiles whipped around, spraying white clouds as they headed west.

The plan was simple, straightforward and very logical. Close down on the KGB cabin from all points on the compass. They had gone over the terrain thoroughly. They had run rehearsals on similar terrain two weeks ago in the Brooks Range. Blake expected to run into some head-on firefighting with the KGB. But the whole strike force expected, indeed, wanted that. These guys had all been blooded in combat plenty of times, and they were always itching for a good fight. A military career was no damn good without an impressive, and hopefully extensive, combat record. Desk jobs and computer war scenarios were for the

WOULD YOU BELIEVE THESE MEN CAN HOLD YOU CAPTIVE IN YOUR OWN HOME?

MAIL THIS STICKER TODAY

WE'LL SEND YOU

4 FREE BOOKS

JUST TO PROVE IT.

See inside for details.

Discover Gold Eagle's power to keep you spellbound . . .

WITHOUT CHARGE OR OBLIGATION

Good books are hard to find. And hard men are good to find. We've got both.

Gold Eagle books are so good, so hard, so exciting that we guarantee they'll keep you riveted to your chair until their fiery conclusion.

That's because you don't just read a Gold Eagle novel . . . you *live* it.

Your blood will race as you join *Mack Bolan* and his high-powered combat squads—*Able Team, Phoenix Force, Vietnam: Ground Zero* and *SOBs*—in their relentless crusade against worldwide terror. You'll feel the pressure build page after page until the nonstop action explodes in a high-voltage climax of vengeance and retribution against mankind's most treacherous criminals.

Get 4 electrifying novels—FREE

To prove Gold Eagle delivers the most pulse-pounding, pressure-packed action reading ever published, we'll send you

4 novels—ABSOLUTELY FREE.

If you like them, we'll send you 6 brand-new books every other month to preview. Always before they're available in stores. Always at a hefty saving off the retail price. Always with the right to cancel and owe nothing.

As a Gold Eagle subscriber, you'll also receive . . .
- our free newsletter, AUTOMAG, with each shipment
- special books to preview free and buy at a deep discount

Get a digital watch—FREE

Return the attached Card today, and we'll also send you a digital quartz calendar watch FREE. It comes complete with a long-life battery and a one-year warranty.

Like the 4 free books, it's yours to keep even if you never buy another Gold Eagle book.

RUSH YOUR ORDER TO US TODAY

Rugged digital quartz calendar watch

Act now, and this versatile timepiece is yours FREE. Easy-to-read LCD display beams exact time, date and running seconds with flawless precision. And the rugged water-resistant styling stands up to the toughest wear.

SEND ME 4 FREE BOOKS AND A FREE WATCH.

YEAH, send my 4 free Gold Eagle novels plus my free watch.

Then send me 6 brand-new Gold Eagle novels (2 *Mack Bolans* and one each of *Able Team*, *Phoenix Force*, *Vietnam: Ground Zero* and *SOBs*) every second month as they come off the presses. Bill me at the low price of $2.49 each (a savings of 13% off the retail price). There are no shipping, handling or other hidden costs. I can always return a shipment and cancel at any time. Even if I never buy a book from Gold Eagle, the 4 free books and the watch are mine to keep.

166 CIM PAJV

Name	(PLEASE PRINT)	
Address		Apt. No.
City	State/Prov.	Zip/Postal Code

Offer limited to one per household and not valid for present subscribers.
Prices subject to change.

**SEND NO MONEY.
MAIL THIS CARD TODAY AND YOU WILL RECEIVE
A SECOND GIFT ABSOLUTELY FREE!**

bozos who would rather suck down Scotch and play grab ass at some bar. The only time a man was really, truly alive, goddammit, Blake thought, was when the lead was flying.

Suddenly the unexpected happened.

Blake watched the gunship as it soared east, away from the LZ. The colonel started to turn his attention away from the chopper when a tremendous explosion sounded in the distance.

Blake and the other members of the CIA fireteam turned, wide-eyed, toward the blazing fireball that boiled over the peaks to the east.

"Son of a..." the colonel heard someone behind him mutter.

An oily black cloud mushroomed over a mountain peak.

If we had flown in from the east... Blake began to think, then stopped himself, as the warped, fiery debris of the gunship plummeted toward the white slope.

Blake thought fast as he felt all eyes turn on him.

"All right, let's move out," he commanded. "I want that firebase. I want a prisoner. Blyleven," he said to the radioman. "Contact those snowmobile teams. Alert them to what's just transpired. Tell them to sit tight near the south gorge until further orders."

"Looks like these Russian bastards want to play hardball, Colonel," Benedict rasped as the team moved out.

"That's just fine with me, Captain," Blake said. "They just threw us a curve, but those people are going to soon find out they're a little out of their league.''

Blake heard a delayed explosion from the gunship wreckage as it echoed throughout the valley.

BOLAN SMASHED THE CABIN DOOR, raked the interior with his mini-Uzi. He hadn't expected to find Strike Force Uncle Sam there, but then again, James Kelly wasn't exactly the parish priest.

"What's the matter, Bolan?" Kelly gloated, standing beside Bolan in the windswept doorway, rotor wash from the Bell blowing funnels of snow around them. "Don't you trust me?"

"Like a tarantula," the warrior in combat whitesuit growled.

"Well, hear this again," Kelly growled back. "Strike Force Uncle Sam is gone. They checked out at 0730. Hell, by now they've probably stormed up that slope, killed every last stinking Russki and recaptured America's two leading scumsuckers. You read that, Bolan? The war, mister, might just be over."

"Think again, Kelly. I've still got Baknov. When this mess is settled, I'm going after that master list."

Bolan looked at Kelly for a moment. The guy had said very little during the three-thousand-mile flight until they hit the border. Then he had opened up like a gutted fish. Rendezvous times. Checkpoints. Precise locations of the strike force safehouse and the KGB cabin that he'd gotten from Intelligence. Yeah, everything in a nutshell. The specialist was playing ball, and Bolan had to wonder why.

The Executioner believed that Kelly was cooperating to save his own skin from his own people. If it looked to the Company that Kelly had helped a one-time CIA target in this operation, a hit team just might go after the specialist for having a loose tongue. The Company played for keeps.

But so did the Executioner.

Bolan gestured toward the gunship with his mini-Uzi. "Move it."

Quickly both men moved away from the cabin, boarded the Bell.

"What's the situation?" Grimaldi wanted to know.

Bolan slid the fuselage door shut. "We're late for the dance. I want to drop Kelly and the Russian off at the town."

Grimaldi looked confused for a moment. "What do you mean? Just drop down in the street and unload."

"You got it, Jack."

"A little obvious, wouldn't you say, Striker?"

"That's the way I want it. In case our birds decide to fly, at least somebody down there will know."

"Roger, big guy," Grimaldi affirmed, lifted off, eased the cyclic stick forward.

"You'd better be straight with me, Kelly," the Executioner warned the agent.

Kelly shrugged. "Like an arrow," he remarked dryly.

Within moments, the Bell was right on top of Taskinoma. A heavy snow cover blanketed the one- and two-story buildings, covered the cars and trucks lining the wide street that bisected the town. Smoke plumed from brick or stone chimneys atop every building. The town appeared to be packed to capacity from what Bolan could tell. And no one appeared anxious to go anywhere.

"Taskinoma's a big whore town, Bolan," Kelly said. "Don't worry about me or the Russian. We won't be going anywhere. For a while," he added, and cracked a thin smile.

"You just make sure you don't go anywhere at any time, Kelly. If I have to come looking for you, it won't be for a ten spot."

"Yeah, yeah, sure," the specialist grumbled.

Grimaldi set the Bell down in the middle of the street.

Bolan slid back the fuselage door. Wind, snow gusted through the Bell.

"Come on, comrade," Kelly gruffed. "Looks like it's me and you."

Bolan watched as Kelly and Baknov disembarked.

Several townsmen appeared on the boardwalk.

"I'll be back," Bolan told Kelly. The Executioner slid the door shut on the specialist and the Soviet defector.

As the gunship lifted off, Kelly and Baknov stood in the middle of the road.

More townsmen gathered on the planks.

Kelly and Baknov looked at each other. Then the specialist looked the town over.

"Vodka, Russian?"

Baknov nodded.

Kelly took Baknov by the arm, led the Soviet defector toward the first establishment that looked like it might have a drink.

KOVEKNY MET KOSYGIN at the bottom of the mountain trail. There, the thirty-five-man KGB killer squad assembled.

Kovekny was pleased with Kosygin's report. The inmates had been turned loose, and a large number of their forces had just been reported moving south, toward the current CIA position.

Kovekny was pleased, but he was not satisfied.

He wondered what was keeping Colonel Belokai. It was more than twelve hours since he'd heard from the assassin. Perhaps Belokai was scheming to take out the CIA gangsters himself. Ambition, Kovekny knew, was an unspoken tradition in the KGB. Officers and agents were always searching for ways to advance, to please their superiors back in Moscow.

As Kovekny studied the tall, young, hard-eyed Kosygin, he knew this officer was anxious to succeed in this skirmish with the CIA. But Kovekny trusted Kosygin about as much as he did Belokai. Ambition often bred deceit. It was easy for a man to become an accomplished liar when he lived inside of his head a good deal of the time. Kovekny decided he'd have to watch Kosygin closely.

Both of them understood fully the consequences of having to return to Moscow in defeat. Without exception, they would all suffer the same fate as Baknov. When the great traitor was recaptured, Kovekny knew, he would be returned immediately to Moscow. There Baknov would be executed after a painful, brutal interrogation. In keeping with Russian tradition, any surviving relatives of Baknov would have to pay for the bullet that would be fired at point-blank range into his brain from behind the ear.

Behind Kovekny and Kosygin, several agents finished burying the bear traps beneath the snow. Whatever pain and shock could be inflicted on the CIA terrormongers would help the KGB win.

Stevhkin stood beside Kosygin. Kovekny noted a look of concern in Stevhkin's eyes as he looked up the slope.

"Is something troubling you, Comrade Stevhkin?"

"*Da*, Comrade Kovekny. You said we were to make it easy for the CIA killers to advance up the trail," Stevhkin pointed out, turning and looking up the three-hundred-foot climb. "Those traps may stop them altogether."

At the top of the trail, perched on the edge of a cliff, sat the cabin. Inside, the two American defectors were bound and gagged.

"Easy, yes, comrade," Kovekny replied. "Easy, that is, for those advancing in the rear. If the Americans make it this far, they will suffer more casualties. They will scream in agony and horror when they realize just how 'easy' their way to the top seems.

"I only suggest that your men are careful, comrades. The entire perimeter has been secured with the bear traps. It was a tactic the CIA used for their safehouse, according to Colonel Belokai."

Kovekny saw the radioman, Anovltky, striding toward him, through the woods. Anovltky's breath plumed out of his mouth like thick white fog. The man was anxious to report some news.

"What is it, comrade?"

"The firebase just reported the CIA has landed in the valley. Exactly where you said they would, comrade."

A smile began to tug at the corners of Kovekny's lips.

"The firebase blew the CIA helicopter out of the sky with the RPGs."

The smile now slashed Kovekny's lips, but vanished as Anovltky continued.

"But the Americans flew in from the south. They disembarked safely at their landing site."

Kovekny drew a deep breath. His expression darkened with somber reflection. The war had begun, just as he had anticipated. The landing zone had been obvious, indeed, a logical choice. Apparently, Anovltky had recounted, the helicopter had been out of rocket range when the CIA gangsters disembarked. The firebase team must have mispositioned themselves somehow. They had secured cover east when they should have set up base to the south. No matter, Kovekny told himself. The aircraft had been destroyed. Certainly, the CIA execution squad would go after the firebase. Kovekny could only hope that his firebase team had the honor to fight to the death, and not be taken prisoners by the Americans.

Kovekny had gone over the intelligence on his CIA counterpart, Colonel Blake. The colonel had an admirable record. For an American. Colonel Blake, Kovekny judged by his record, was a fighting man of grim resolve. Kovekny believed that one's strength, one's success in battle could only be measured by the ability of one's adversary. The stronger the opponent, the better.

"Very well, comrade," Kovekny told Anovltky. "Keep me informed by the half hour."

Then, Kovekny turned to address Kosygin and Stevhkin. "Assemble your teams. Move out and take up positions."

"And what of Colonel Belokai?" Kosygin wanted to know. "He ordered us to wait until he arrived."

Anger sparked in Kovekny's eyes. "Comrade Kosygin, I am in charge here, until the colonel arrives or until I am dead. Do you understand?"

Kosygin was slow in replying. "Certainly, Comrade Kovekny. I understand perfectly."

Kovekny's stern gaze lingered on Kosygin. Suddenly, Kovekny had the feeling that this battle was about to become every man for himself.

It was unsettling.
The cold mountain air seemed to bite at his face.
Like a viper, he thought.
Poised to strike.
Eager to kill.

11

There was no love lost between Colonel Thomas Blake and the self-styled ace of the midnight sun.

The colonel felt nothing for the gunship's dead pilot.

But an American was an American. And Blake still owed his loyalty to the Stars and Stripes.

Soviet heads were going to roll.

Communist treachery and brutality deserved nothing better than death, the colonel thought.

Yeah, Blake enjoyed killing Communists almost as much as he did Muslims. In fact, it was often difficult for him to decide which group he enjoyed killing more. The colonel often fantasized about flying over Mecca in an F-16. Just laying waste the whole stinking Islamic capital right after a good lunch and a Camel unfiltered. Of course, the Jews would love him for that, and that was no good, he decided. But he would deal with the glory afterward. Then it would be on to Moscow and Leningrad. He would whistle while he bombed. Something by Beethoven or Wagner. He knew how much the Russkis loved the Germans. The Russians had a long history of getting their asses handed to them by the Germans, but, then again, so had all of Europe. And, in reality, the only thing that had kept the Germans from tearing down the gates of Moscow in World War II had been the Allies occupying a good deal of Nazi attention back on the European front.

Indeed, he thought, if he could roll all Communists and Muslims up into one big ball, he'd have a mountain of human feces on his hands bigger than Mount McKinley. Yeah, there was plenty of killing to keep him busy for a hundred lifetimes.

And the only thing better than fantasizing about dealing out death to the scum of the world, was doing it in the flesh and blood.

Now was one of those times.

The KGB firebase team consisted of four killers. Two Soviets lugged the RPG-7s that had downed the American gunship. The other two KGB butchers, Blake saw, carried RPK-74s. Damn heavy firepower. The Russians weren't there to talk about Geneva. When first spotting the Russian team scurrying through the deep cover of the woods, the colonel had formulated this initial leg of the killhunt.

Half of Blake's force had gone ahead to intercept the Russians. Blake and Captain Benedict's unit would close on the Russians from behind, drive them on ahead into the death wedge.

A scissors attack, Blake thought. Instant annihilation. It had worked dozens of times on search and destroy missions for him and his Skull and Crossbones squad in Nam.

At the moment the Russians were still unaware that they were being stalked.

Silently, swiftly, Blake and his executioners shadowed through the woods. If the Russians spotted them now they would certainly turn their RPGs loose. The colonel had ordered his team to use their own LAWs only as a last resort.

Blake wanted a prisoner in the worst way. But he would shred these Russki butchers if he had to.

The Russian walking point suddenly stopped. And called the action.

"Damn!" Blake muttered.

The Russian indicated the shadows pursuing them from behind. He yelled an order to his comrades. The RPG couple swung the launchers atop their shoulders and opened up on the Americans.

But the other half of Blake's slaughter force converged on the Russians, M-16s blazing from the gloom of the slope ahead of the doomed Soviet invaders.

In less than a second, Blake witnessed his plan succeeding with grim, deadly finality.

The KGB team was caught like fish in a net by the lightning pincer attack. American autofire cut them down in a cross fire hurricane of 7.62 NATO lead. A missile belched away from one of the RPGs. But the Russian had already gone down in crimson tatters, and the aim was thrown skyward. An explosion then rocked the forest floor as the projectile erupted against the side of a cliff, fifty yards behind Blake.

The CIA squad surrounded the fallen Russians.

"Anybody hit?" Blake asked, checking his troops.

Everyone was unharmed, accounted for.

Blake turned dark attention to the slaughterbed.

Only one Russian survived the murderous assault. His guts were now leaking out into the snow, and he was fast losing his grip on life.

Blake was disappointed. But he had learned his lessons in torture well from the glory days of Vietnam. A little pain went a long way in loosening a prisoner's tongue.

"Okay, potato face," the colonel rasped, looming over the dying Russian.

A horrible wheezing blew past the Russian's blood-flecked lips. He coughed up blood.

"Where are the rest of your comrades?" Blake asked.

The Russian was slow in answering. Blake squeezed off a 3-round burst, punching holes in the snow around the Russian's head.

"I can make it quick for you, comrade," Blake said, his eyes blazing, aiming the snout of his M-16A2 at the Russian's agony-twisted features. "Or, I can leave you for the wolves to finish off."

Blake knew the numbers of the KGB force. Thirty-five, minus three. Soon to be minus four. But the colonel wanted to know the enemy's exact position, their strategy.

He had already lost close to four hours in this hunt. And his patience had long since been replaced by a dangerous time bomb of rage.

The Russian injected defiant hatred into his eyes. "I . . . I tell you n-nothing. . . ."

Captain Benedict got into the act. "Think again," he snarled, kicked the Russian's wound. "You just killed two men in that bird. You'll die long and hard, comrade, unless you answer the colonel's questions."

A strangled laugh sounded in the Russian's throat. "Wh-what is it . . . you Americans say? Go fuck yourself?"

Benedict buried his foot in the Russian's gut.

The man's scream shrilled through the forest.

"Hell, let's get on with it, Colonel," Benedict said. "This guy's just killing time. His own."

"One last chance, comrade."

Blake waited. The Russian appeared to think about something for a moment.

"I will tell y-you this much. . . . You Americans will all be d-dead before you hit the top of . . . the trail. . . ."

"What trail?" Blake demanded. "The trail to the cabin where you're holding Snipes and Dover?"

The Russian forced a smile, winced. The light began to fade in his eyes. "D-dead men . . . all . . ."

"Yeah, right, comrade," Blake growled. "Say hello to Stalin for me. In hell," he said, then fired a burst, erasing the Russian's face.

"They got something planned, Colonel," Benedict quickly said, the killing shots trailing off into the woods. "Sounds like they've maybe mined that trail."

"Could be," Blake allowed, thinking. If his team met no resistance on the way to the cabin, he thought, then the Russians had definitely laid some sort of trap. What had the KGB planned? What waited for the Americans next? The only Russian Blake liked and trusted was a dead one.

And there would be plenty more dead Russians before the day was over, he swore to himself. Or he would spend one long, cold, hard night living up to that promise.

He hadn't come to the far dark end of the North American continent just to parley for an exchange of defectors.

No damn way.

This was his war.

"Let's move it out. Three teams. Eagle Wing formation," the colonel told his killteam, and led his warriors into the black heart of the forest.

And a fire of its own burned in Blake's heart.

He had only just begun to take that fire to the Communist bastards.

"WHAT THE HELL'S all the whinin' about?" Milt Freeman rasped at the Long Knives huddled together in the fuselage behind him.

Freeman felt his irritation edging toward rage. Since leaving behind the volcanic eye of Mount Saint Helens, his troops had sounded like a bunch of snot-nosed schoolkids bitching about having to hold their bowels for another ten miles.

No, he had no idea when they would get to their destination. No, he had no idea even what that destination was. And yes, it was all a risk. Everything. From radar tracking of the target vessel to finding the actual zone of the firefight. And yes, he would hand somebody their balls if they took a leak in the chopper.

"The boys are just getting a little restless for some action, Snake, is all," Joe Lala said.

Sure, Freeman thought. And I'm not?

With the chopper's long-range radar, the Long Knives had trailed the Bell all the way across the States and into Canada. Frequent fuel stops by the target helicopter had helped Freeman's pilots keep within radar range of the enemy aircraft. Whether or not the target chopper was equipped with its own radar, Freeman wasn't sure. If the butchers of his fellow Long Knives had picked up their progress on radar, Freeman assumed they would simply turn around and fight it out in the sky, dogfight style. Except that their twin-turbine choppers were not armed with rocket pods and miniguns. A dogfight would have been no contest. Still, Freeman had ordered his pilots to stick close to the target, gambling that the enemy had bigger things on their minds than slugging it out in midair.

The gamble had paid off. So far.

Now all Freeman had to do was find the bastards.

Checking his map, and relying on his pilot's control panel, Freeman believed they were somewhere over the Alaska Range.

Moments later, Freeman spotted the summit of Mount McKinley, perhaps eight to ten miles northwest.

A towering monolith of granite, washed in snow, ringed by mist, seemed to part the horizon, open up the slate-gray sky.

"Look at that, will ya," Pete Simms breathed, staring awestruck off into the distance. "Hell, Snake, if we don't get ourselves a war with those Russians, maybe we oughta buy some climbing gear and top that baby out. Man, I've always wanted to scale a rock like that."

"Yeah, well, do it on your own time, okay," Freeman growled. "I didn't bring you dudes on no three-thousand-mile ride just so you could catch the sights."

"Wait a minute."

Freeman turned an intent stare on Weebie Jordan, whose high-powered field glasses were pressed up against the window of the cockpit bubble.

"What is it?" Freeman asked.

"Movement. Down there in the woods. And they ain't no caribou, Snake. I got a force of maybe twenty guys. All with rifles."

"Lemme have those glasses."

"Hold on, Snake," Jordan said, swinging the glasses left. "I got something on fire down there.

Looks like wreckage. A hull, man. Could be that chopper we been tracking.''

Freeman grabbed the glasses out of Jordan's hands, scoured the earth. ''I'll be damned.''

The leader of the Long Knives lowered the glasses. Snake Eyes Freeman was sure that the blackened heap of junk on the valley floor was the target aircraft. Target, yeah, he thought. Target terminated. He liked that phrase. He liked to use the words target and terminate as often as possible. That was how they talked in the CIA. Spook speak. He had read that somewhere in a mercenary rag.

''Drop her down,'' he ordered the pilot. ''I wanna take a look. Radio the other chopper. Same thing.'' Excitement built in Freeman's voice as he turned, addressed the dozen men crammed together around him. ''This is it. This is war. This is what we've been training for years to go up against. We're all in this thing. We take the fight straight to these people. War, dammit, war! This is where we start to make a name for ourselves.''

They stared back at him, and for a second Freeman wondered if any of them comprehended what he was saying.

''Hell, do you dudes understand what I'm sayin'?''

Nods. Grunts.

''Right on, bro,'' Sam Pip said.

''We're in this all the way, Snake,'' Lala added. ''We didn't come no three thousand miles to let some Russians kick our asses.''

Freeman nodded. "All right, then. That's what I like to hear."

But somehow his own voice sounded hollow to his ears.

Freeman wasn't so sure he liked the way he'd heard those words of bravado.

No, he wasn't at all sure.

Those voices lacked balls.

GRIMALDI LOOKED UP from the radar screen, turned and told Bolan, "We've got company ahead, Striker. Two aircraft. Just over the next ridge."

Bolan checked the rugged, mountainous terrain through his binoculars. A wall of formidable rock showed to the north and to the east. But Bolan spotted a narrow gorge between those rock barriers.

Passage.

But to what?

"Close enough, Jack. Drop it down in that ravine. I don't want my company to know they have a guest coming."

Grimaldi guided the Bell into the mouth of the ravine, then landed the whirlybird. A little less than a hundred yards ahead, a patch of fog boiled in the eastern mouth of the gorge, hiding the valley beyond to Bolan's immediate surveillance.

Bolan's thermal combat whitesuit was loaded down for war. Silenced Beretta 93-R nestled snug in its speed rig beneath his left arm. Big Thunder hung in quick-draw leather strapped low to his right thigh. Mini-Uzi strapped around his neck. Four frag grenades. Commando knife sheathed just above his left hip. Garrote. And spare clips for all hardware.

The Executioner planned to slam firepower first into this CIA-KGB war.

Firepower first, damn right.

The dice were loaded.

And Bolan was ready to roll those dice.

Winner take all.

"You really expect that Kelly to sit tight, Striker?" Grimaldi asked.

"He'll keep, Jack. I wanted to give the guy just enough rope. He's still a soldier on the same side we are. Whatever else Kelly is, time, and this war will tell. Something tells me he wants to wait this out, see who's left standing."

"King of the mountain, yeah," Grimaldi growled. "I read the guy like that, too. The CIA wins, he'll be the first one running to them with open arms, and his Comrade Baknov. The KGB wins, he deals himself out of this. I don't trust the son of a bitch."

"He'd be excess baggage out here, Jack. Worse, the minute he saw his people he'd squall loud enough to shake the walls back at Langley."

"And nothing but hot air," the ace pilot said. "Hey, listen, if that guy lied to you about any of this, Striker, you could be walking right into the guns."

Bolan pulled up his hood. "Personally, I just couldn't believe somebody would do something like that," he dryly remarked.

Grimaldi shook his head softly, crooked a smile at the big warrior. "This game's full of liars, Striker. That's the only way either side can deal with reality and each other, it seems. Hell, you've seen it."

Bolan looked at his friend for a moment. Sadness stabbed Bolan. Yeah, he'd seen the treachery, all right, many times. And he would never forget.

The haunted look in Bolan's eyes was read right away by Grimaldi.

"Sorry, guy," the pilot quietly said. "I didn't mean to sound so damn callous."

It took a second for Grimaldi's voice to break through Bolan's reflection. He chucked Grimaldi on the shoulder, opened the cockpit door.

"Hey, hold on."

Bolan jumped out of the cockpit, turned and looked back at Grimaldi.

"Hell, I know you don't just want me to sit here and daydream. How about some recon? How about some fire support? You might need a quick evac."

Bolan patted the bulge where the radio handset was concealed. "I'll be in touch. Air recon, I might need. I'll check in with you on the hour."

Grimaldi gave Bolan a thumbs-up. "Good luck, big guy."

Bolan closed the door.

He gave the rimrock high above him a quick but thorough surveillance.

Then the Executioner moved out.

To find a war.

To execute two traitors.
And to roll a whole lot of black dice.
The wild card of Death vanished into the fog.

12

From the window of the twin-turbine Bell 222, Colonel Lev Belokai spotted the positions of the Russian hit teams through his binoculars. Five-man squads strategically placed along the crests of the southern range. A two-man sniper team with silenced Dragunovs had secured cover behind rimrock overlooking a deep gorge.

Kovekny had already deployed the execution squads. That told Belokai the CIA gangsters were advancing.

The KGB colonel felt the blood rushing hot through his face. His stomach knotted with a rising anger. He was late for the war. Kovekny was giving orders in his absence.

But Comrade Kovekny was ambitious, Belokai knew. Kovekny was a hungry agent. He wanted recognition by Moscow. The man was a vain, pompous fool if he believed he would secure a higher place for himself in the Committee's hierarchy once victory over the CIA was final and decisive.

Kovekny was nothing more than a subordinate, a mere peasant from the outskirts of Velikiy Ustyug. But he had served well in the military as a draftee. Later, as a lower-ranking officer in the KGB, he had shown initiative at stations in India and Afghanistan. Still, the man was too ambitious for Colonel Belokai's liking.

Belokai decided to straighten matters out with the arrogant Kovekny. As soon as the helicopter landed.

The colonel turned, his dark gaze narrowing as he looked at the American pilot he had bought and paid for. Twenty-five thousand dollars had won the pilot's service. Temporarily. The pilot was expendable. Like rubbish. Belokai had promised him an additional twenty-five thousand dollars once they reached their destination. The American was a fool. How easily bought these people were, Belokai thought. For a few easy dollars they would do anything. Including selling out their own people. Capitalism was most certainly doomed to extinction, Belokai thought. Money controlled the capitalists' every move. Greed was simply an inherent part of the western culture. Greed was the lifeblood of these people, Belokai thought. The NATO alliance had been living well and easy since the end of the Great Patriotic War.

But those days were numbered. The capitalist system was ripe for conquest by the hungry, the strong.

One system would have to perish in order for the entire world to continue to exist. There was simply no compromising in this war between communism and capitalism. Not with the stakes being the entire world. Not with the question of nuclear war hovering like a black cloud over the heads of every seat of government in the world.

The American fools actually believed they could call the Russian premier to this Geneva summit. They actually believed Russia would back down because of this new American threat, SDI, and that the Kremlin would order the disarmament of some ridiculous number of nuclear warheads.

It was all talk, Belokai knew.

It was all to appease the fools who dreamed of peace. Who dreamed of a world without nuclear weapons.

The Americans and their NATO puppets were clearly, blindly stupid. Their naïveté would be their undoing.

Behind Belokai sat Dmivsky and Chaadeyev. The colonel glanced at his two underlings. All of them had ridden out the long flight in silence. Dmivsky and Chaadeyev knew better than to question any of his decisions, Belokai thought. They had done exactly as they were told back in West Virginia. They had not questioned the doomed assault against the CIA in the town of Lee's Crossing. They had not questioned their colonel's solo reconnaissance of the dummy CIA safehouse where Belokai had first encountered Mack Bolan.

And Belokai's mind had wandered frequently toward thoughts of the Executioner. Of course, Belokai had felt it his duty to radio ahead and warn Kovekny of possible Bolan intervention. No, not possible, certain and absolute interference in the war by the man known as the Executioner.

Kovekny had sounded skeptical at the news.

Belokai felt the comforting weight of the Kukri in its scabbard. It was a formidable and beautiful weapon. He was anxious to use it again. And again. He decided that when he beheaded Bolan, the Executioner, like some ceremonial Dushera ox, he would leave the blood on the sixteen-inch blade until he returned to Moscow.

Belokai had spent the greater part of his adult life serving the motherland. He had earned the right, the privilege, to claim a decisive victory against the CIA here in the Alaskan wilderness.

For the glory of the State!

The CIA gangsters would feel the superior strength of the KGB. Certainly, there would be some leak in CIA intelligence, Belokai thought. A leak that would spill to the American public all information about the KGB victory over the imperialist warmongers. That would be the ultimate humiliation.

Vietnam.

Iran.

Belokai always felt a jolt of excitement whenever he thought about those American failures. About the respect the imperialist lackeys had lost in the eyes of the world.

And just look at how vulnerable they were to international terrorism, Belokai thought, and fought down the laughter. Not only were they vulnerable to attacks by international criminals, but they never retaliated. Well, except for the air assault on Libya. What sort of insanity was that. The KGB had anti-terrorist execution squads on constant standby just in case a diplomat was killed, or an embassy was assaulted. The Committee would not hesitate to strike back against these international thugs.

Moscow was still chuckling about the aborted hostage rescue mission in Iran. Even five years after the fact.

"You want me to set this bird down, comrade?"

Anger flickered through Belokai's eyes. "Yes, of course." Idiot, he thought as he looked at the transport truck parked on the clearing to the south of the cabin.

There Kovekny waited with Stevhkin. As the helicopter descended toward the LZ, Belokai saw the silenced Dragunovs and the AKMs he had requested.

When the chopper landed Belokai flung open the door, stepped out, returned the salutes of Kovekny and Stevhkin.

"Report," Belokai ordered.

"The American CIA team landed in a valley ten kilometers south," Kovekny said. "Our firebase shot down their helicopter, but after the Americans disembarked."

Belokai looked closely at Kovekny. His use of "our firebase" displeased Belokai. He decided he did not like this officer.

"Go on."

Kovekny cleared his throat. "It is believed that our firebase has either been captured or eliminated by the CIA."

"Believed?"

"Yes, Comrade Colonel. They have not reported in more than two hours."

Belokai felt the tension tie a knot in his chest. The firebase team had been eliminated, he was sure. He cursed silently. Casualties already.

"Go on," Belokai ordered.

"Our perimeter has been secured by our teams as you ordered, Comrade Colonel." A sly smile touched Kovekny's lips. "The American defectors are bound and gagged inside the cabin."

Belokai looked up at the cabin, several hundred feet above at the top of the cliff.

"Our plan is to make the trail to the cabin seem as easy as possible for the Americans. As you ordered, Comrade Colonel, the way has cleverly been made difficult by the bear traps. Upon your orders, a team will be placed halfway down the slope beside the trail to monitor the CIA advance. If, comrade, they get this far."

"You will see to it that they do, Comrade Kovekny. As many of them as possible."

"I understand, Comrade Colonel."

"And the cabin itself?"

"Lined with crates of plastic explosive, as ordered." Kovekny smiled again. "Two hundred pounds."

Kovekny hesitated again. And Belokai found himself becoming greatly annoyed with the officer. Kovekny was waiting to be prodded for answers by his superior officer.

"And?"

"The institute, Jarkin, was attacked early this morning. Comrade Kosygin set all inmates free. They were given the Metaclyn. They should be advancing now toward the town, Taskinoma. There will be considerable chaos and murder there. If the CIA has planned to bring in any outside forces it is hoped that the diversionary attack on the town will lure them there. Or, if the CIA has a backup team waiting there..."

"Yes, yes, I know the details. And I know why I gave you those orders, comrade. I noticed," Belokai said, scowling as the icy blast of snow swirled around him beneath the Bell's rotor wash, "that you saw fit to deploy our teams."

"We could not wait for your return, Comrade Colonel. My apologies."

The man was sniveling, Belokai thought. A vain attempt to ingratiate himself with a superior.

"Has there been any sign of the man Bolan?" Belokai asked. The KGB killer felt his anger edging toward rage when Kovekny looked at him quizzically.

"No, Comrade Colonel."

"You act as if you do not believe what I tell you."

"No, Comrade Colonel. I only know that there has been no sighting of Bolan."

"Hey, uh, begging your pardon there, comrade."

Belokai snapped his head sideways, his chilling gaze coming to rest on the American pilot in the doorway of the helicopter cockpit. Belokai saw a silly, frightened expression on the pilot's face.

"Say, uh, I gotta be goin', comrade. I flew you people here and all, and it's been great. But you owe me twenty-five grand still."

Belokai drew a deep breath, felt the frosty mountain air burn his windpipe. His hands folded behind his back, he glanced at Kovekny and Stevhkin, then returned his attention back to the pilot.

"Yes, you have done well," Belokai told the pilot. "And your services will be much appreciated by the Kremlin."

"Hey, look, buddy, this ain't something I'll be bragging about in my hometown. C'mon, let's square this tab. I gotta go."

Belokai reached into the pocket of his black leather trench coat and withdrew a thick, folded wad of hundred-dollar bills. He gestured at the pilot with the money, beckoned. "Please. Step out."

The pilot hesitated, then shook his head, muttered, "Jesus."

Belokai stood patiently, holding the money as the pilot stepped out of the cockpit. The Russian handed the pilot the money.

The pilot whistled, his fingers riffling the edges of the crisp bills. "For a bunch of guys who hate us imperialist capitalist pigs so much, you sure can pay for services rendered. None of that check-in-the-mail bullshit.''

Belokai smiled.

The pilot smiled.

"And thank you, comrade, for those services rendered,'' Belokai said, reaching inside his trench coat.

The American chopper pilot looked Belokai in the eye, smiling.

"And *do svidaniya*," Belokai growled, his smile twisting into a feral snarl.

"Yeah, and *do svid*..."

Belokai plunged the Kukri into the pilot's stomach with such force he lifted the American an inch off the ground. The bills flew away from the pilot's hand, scattered by the furious wind of the rotor wash. The pilot's hands twitched as he convulsed, reaching for the embedded Kukri.

Belokai stared into the shock and agony that bulged the pilot's eyes. The colonel twisted on the blade, wrenched up on the handle, slicing open the pilot from navel to breastbone. Blood gushed from the cavernous wound, splashed the snow around Belokai's boots. The pilot jerked, slumped back against the cockpit door.

The KGB officers surrounding Belokai showed no emotion. They stood motionless, silent.

The pilot's deadweight finally pulled him free of the tempered, razor-sharp blade.

Belokai held the blade out for a moment. His mask of rage melted into an impassive expression as the corpse toppled to the snow.

Then the assassin stooped. Repeatedly, he wiped the blade on the pilot's pant legs until he could clearly see the *Ordep Nepal*, the seal of acceptance on the steel. When he was satisfied with the appearance of the Kukri, Belokai sheathed the British Gurkha military knife.

The KGB officers who had just witnessed the brutal murder appeared as if they didn't dare move.

Belokai turned, addressed the agents under his command. "That, comrades, is the only way to dispose of garbage."

Twenty-five thousand American dollars swirled around Lev Belokai.

WHEN GRIMALDI SPOTTED the weapon-wielding mob surging across the snowfield, warning bells sounded in his head. Aerial recon, he knew, had just turned up a very important sighting.

And a very dangerous discovery. Beyond the shadow of a doubt.

As he soared over the tide of fur-coated men and women, he took in their strange variety of arms. AK-47s. Axes. Meat cleavers. Pitchforks.

What the hell was going on?

According to his map there was no town in any direction for miles.

Bolan had to know about this development. But Grimaldi didn't dare break radio silence. The big guy could be stalking the KGB killers at that moment.

Grimaldi decided to take a closer look. He reversed the Bell in a hairpin turn, then flew back over the mob.

For a moment, he held the chopper at a hover. The mob kept advancing, oblivious, it seemed, to the aircraft.

They moved almost like wooden fixtures, Grimaldi thought, and heard the alarm bells ringing louder, like zombies.

No, more like mindless animals.

Like dead men.

Grimaldi set the chopper down.

The tide of zombies surged toward his LZ.

He glimpsed the wild-eyed look in the hollow rings of several faces. Then someone in the group opened up on him with an AK-47. The mob swept over the Bell like a pack of rabid animals.

Weapons pounded the cockpit doors. A baseball bat hammered off the Plexiglas.

Grimaldi lifted the whirlybird, saw a man clinging to the skids. Autofire blazed from below, hot lead dancing off the bulletproof bubble.

Grimaldi watched as the guy lost his grip on the skid, plunged toward the mob.

The ace pilot spotted something ahead, near the outer fringes of the woods. Lumps, they looked like to Grimaldi.

Moments later, he discovered those lumps were the slaughtered carcasses of a caribou herd. Grimaldi hovered over the carnage. Near that bloody deathbed he saw the hacked-up, gutted corpses of two men. Their sheepskin coats were a dark crimson smear against the white of the snow. Their knives lay just beyond their splayed fingers.

What the hell was this insanity? Grimaldi wondered, his stare dark, grim. Who were those people? They appeared seized by some murderous rage.

Yeah, appeared, all right.

Drugged. That had to be the answer, Grimaldi decided.

But why?

And who had drugged them? CIA? KGB?

Were the crazies townsmen? Prisoners?

Questions jostled for position in Grimaldi's mind.

He had to get some hard answers fast, then fill Bolan in.

The tide of lunatics was fast closing down on the zone.

On the Executioner's position.

Grimaldi got a sick feeling in the pit of his belly.

The snow-covered slopes of this mountain range were going to run red with blood.

There was more than one war to be fought here.

13

Bolan kept to the woods that ringed the valley's fortresslike gorges. Silently and swiftly, he cut through the swirling mist, a phantom in whitesuit. For the moment, the Executioner had opted to go with the silenced Beretta 93-R. The numbers were not tallied, and he could be stepping feetfirst into a pit of vipers.

There was really no telling who would turn the guns on him.

But Bolan had no intention of fighting it out with the CIA team. No, they were all supposed to be soldiers on the same side, damn right. Still, his presence on the zone would be damned by them.

So the Executioner's penetration had to be as silent and as invisible as the breeze. Just the same, if the numbers tumbled in one hellfire fury, Little Lightning would fill his fist in a heartbeat. He would roll the black dice, and punch any hostile numbers a 9 mm parabellum snake eye.

Since the CIA had seen fit to hire free-lancers, thus disavowing any responsibility for or knowledge of the Alaskan war with the KGB, Bolan had a pretty good idea about what sort of "soldiers on the same side" he might be encountering. Mercenaries. Ex-military men. Professional assassins. Men who, essentially, sold their souls to the highest lord of Death.

House rules in the merc world meant top dollar bought all loyalties. Good, bad and filthy dirty.

It was dirty war, yeah.

But Mack Bolan understood that the CIA could not fight on terms that were anything less than dirty and ruthless. And no, they could not, as Bolan had recently heard some senator say, "negotiate for a peaceful settlement," with the goddamn cannibals. When legislators started talking that kind of tripe they were blinding themselves to the grim reality of life. There were real, bona fide enemies of mankind in the world. There was such a thing as evil. There were those who would topple the governments of the free world and impose their own tyrannical will on those under their domination.

Without a doubt, it was a very thin veil that the Khaddafis, the Khomeinis and the Arafats of the world wore. Animal man wanted power, complete domination. The United States and NATO had become the convenient puppet enemy of evil men simply because they were top dog. The Muslim fanatics could spout on about the sovereign will of Allah all they wanted. The Communists could rave about the evils of capitalism all they wanted.

Bolan knew exactly what it was that the scum wanted.

They wanted the world. And conquering the world, or even a small portion of it, required slaughtering a whole lot of people. Innocent people.

Once again, Bolan found himself at war against the Hydra.

They came in the form of the KGB.

Perhaps, Bolan thought, this might just be a skirmish, a bloody prelude to an Armageddon showdown. But somehow he doubted that. He would stop the KGB here, yeah. He would execute the traitors, Snipes and Dover.

Then, he would go after that master list.

Activities and names. Worldwide.

A global search and destroy of KGB killers and their crony terrorist forces.

The silence that hung over the broad, misty valley weighed down on Bolan. He checked the snowfield, moving on quickly. A herd of caribou loped across the plain. That was something else he might have to watch for, too, he thought. Animals. Already he had encountered a number of tracks. This was not only caribou land, but grizzly and wolf country, as well. It was possible, Bolan decided, that the KGB had booby-trapped the perimeter of their defense position with steel jaws normally meant to snare wild beasts.

A different and more deadly game was now in play.

Moving past a stream that tumbled out of the mist, Bolan closed down on the burning wreckage of the gunship. Ahead, the crackling flames, the oily black smoke, parted the white fog like a beacon.

There wasn't enough left of the gunship to get a positive make on it, but Bolan had to assume it was the bird that had transported the CIA killteam. It was unlikely the Soviets would be flying around American airspace in a Mi-28/HAVOC, or any other helicopter gunship.

Bolan found plenty of tracks near the wreckage. Manmade tracks, this time. Perhaps dozens, but he didn't stop to count the telltale signs of life. He did note that one set of tracks intermingled with another. As if two parties had converged on the gunship ruins from different directions. Or as if a second party had stumbled on the debris after the first. After Grimaldi's finding on the radar screen prior to his disembarkment on the LZ, Bolan decided the latter was the logical assumption.

Checking his chronometer, Bolan found he was approaching his check-in time with Grimaldi.

He gave it another fifteen minutes of dogging the tracks, then reached for his radio handset. But he froze, suddenly spotting the blood-drenched, bullet-ravaged bodies. Moving cautiously, Bolan checked the uniforms beneath the whitesuits. Dark green. KGB. Most likely the KGB firebase team that had blown the gunship out of the sky.

Except that Bolan could see that the KGB unit had been stripped of whatever firepower they had carried.

By target party number one or two? he wondered.

Whichever, the hellhounds had gathered on the slopes.

Blood was the lure.

Death would be the ultimate prize.

Bolan radioed Grimaldi. "Ground zero to Striker, come in."

The radio crackled for a second in Bolan's hand. Then Grimaldi's voice came over the airwaves. The Executioner instantly detected the note of anxiety in his pilot's tone.

"We've got a situation here, ground zero. Ten klicks due north of your drop-off site."

"Fill me in, Jack."

"I don't know what to make of it, Striker. A pack of kill-crazy men and women. Armed to the goddamned teeth. Everything from AK-47s to butcher knives. I dropped down to get a closer look, but was forced away when they opened up on me with autofire. They all looked to be drugged, but I'll be damned if I know what that drug is.

"Found a herd of caribou a hundred yards beyond the mob. Two of their own people, also, it looked like. Man and animal gutted and hacked up.

"There's no town on the map, Striker, for maybe a hundred miles in any direction. In other words, there's just not supposed to be anybody out here."

Bolan puzzled over Grimaldi's intel for a moment. A weapon-wielding mob of drugged lunatics?

"Do you think it's some kind of KGB ploy, Striker?"

"Bet on it," the Executioner said. "Why, and from where those people came, I couldn't tell you, Jack."

"Okay, I read you loud and clear, guy. I'll get on it. How are the ground troops?"

"No sighting of any targets yet. But I've come across a KGB team. All of them dead. There's a gunship, probably a Huey that I left behind. Smoked out of the sky. I'd say the war's started. I want to silence radio contact between us, Jack. Unless it's an absolute emergency, don't try to make contact. I don't want any unfriendlies homing in on this frequency. I'm going in."

"Got it, Striker. What about a rendezvous?"

Bolan checked his watch. He had to allow himself ample time to get into the heart of the zone. And if it was man stalking man up and down the wooded, snow-drenched slopes, then that might require some time to complete this search and destroy. And Bolan had to allow for any unforeseen variables. Prisoners taken by the other side. Retreat by enemy numbers. Scattered forces. Or perhaps when the heat of the firefight neared them, the Soviets would move their American traitors somewhere deeper in the range.

"Eight hours, Jack. Same drop-off site."

"Roger that, Striker. Over and out."

Bolan killed radio contact.

Damn, he thought, just what the hell had the KGB butchers done? Drug-crazed psychos? If they were marching his way, then Bolan knew he would run into them. Sooner or later. He would have to.

All targets now became unknown, unidentified.

And unpredictability now rode the edge of hell.

Bolan wondered about Taskinoma as he forged ahead into the foggy gloom of the forest. What if the KGB meant for that mob to attack the town?

Bolan unslung the mini-Uzi from around his neck.

The war was upon him.

And he was headed right into some caldron of blind insanity.

WHEN MILT FREEMAN STOPPED, turned around and saw Otis Borton sucking from his pint of whiskey, he damn near blew that bottle right out of the man's hand. It was the third time during the past hour he'd warned Borton about "drinking on the job." Strike three should have meant Freeman blowing the bottle out of Borton's hand along with half of his face and head. It was bad enough Borton was a stinking drunk, and a hothead to boot. But Freeman was smart enough to realize that if he shot and killed the son of a bitch he would have a mutiny on his hands.

Freeman did the only thing he could. He snatched the pint out of Borton's hands and hurled it into the woods.

Anger and confusion immediately froze Borton's features. "What the—"

"Shut up!" Freeman snarled. He noticed that his assault force was again bunching up around and behind him. Just like he'd told them not to do. Five years of training, Snake Eyes thought bitterly, shot to hell on their first big mission together.

Freeman looked at Jordon as the big man crouched beside him. Even his *segundo* looked green to him at the moment. Green as puke.

"Hey," Freeman rasped at his troops. "I've told you to keep spread out. We stay bunched like this, one good volley of autofire will cut us all to fucking ribbons."

Jordon ignored Freeman's outburst. The *segundo*'s attention was turned toward the valley below the advancing Long Knives. Because of the enshrouding mist, there was no telling how high the granite peaks to the north reached. A clear field of vision was limited to three hundred yards, down the immediate slope and into the valley. There, at the bottom of the incline, a flat snowy blanket stretched to the other side of the valley. Timber slopes ringed the plain.

"All right, listen to me," Freeman growled. "Joe," he said to Lala, "I want you to take a group, head down and move straight across the valley."

"That's all open ground down that way, Snake," Lala complained. "What if there's snipers up in the rock on the other side?"

Freeman scowled. If there were snipers, then Freeman intended to find that out. He figured Lala and his boys could make it to the other side without suffering too many casualties. Sometimes sacrifices had to be made during war so that the group as a whole had a chance at survival. That piece of reasoning, of course, would never get relayed to any of the Long Knives. Freeman wasn't there for any grandstand heroics.

Lonely is the hunter, yeah, he thought, but he intended to live to tell about the triumph of the Long Knives back in his home state. There was no glory in dying.

"Look, Joey," Freeman said, lowering his voice, "that patch of flatland is maybe a hundred yards across from where we're sitting."

"How can you tell?" Lala growled. "With that fog blanket it could be another hundred yards to the other side."

Freeman shook his head. "C'mon, Joey. This isn't some bullshit game we're playing, man. That fog down there will cover you. Just take a look!"

For a second, Freeman thought Lala was going to say, If that's so, why don't you do it?

But Freeman knew Lala's pride would step in. No, Joe Lala believed himself to be a man's man, a ladies' man. There was no way he would come across as anything less than superhuman to the rest of the Long Knives.

"All right, Snake," Lala said.

"You'll be covered the whole way," Freeman assured. "Me and Weebie and the boys'll move east through the woods. I'll radio in one of our choppers. We've got a sniper team that'll cover you from the air. It'll be a piece of cake. Now, pick your boys."

Lala grunted, turned to choose the men he would take.

"COLONEL," Captain Benedict said, looking through his 10x50 binocs, "I don't know who these guys are, but they're advancing hard on our rear and left flank. Four hundred yards south."

Colonel Thomas Blake turned, looked through his own binoculars. True to what Benedict had relayed, two groups were moving down the southern slope to the south. One group of perhaps sixteen men marched through the wooded slopes. Another group of ten men moved across the frozen surface of the lake. As they cleared the cover of fog patches, Blake made out the cowboy and black rebel hats. He saw one guy, who couldn't have stood any more than five feet tall, leading his force through the woods.

Christ, Blake angrily thought, that's all I need now. A pint-sized good ol' boy with a Napoleonic complex and a chip on his shoulder probably as high as Mount McKinley.

A bitter sigh rasped through Blake's lips. His main fireteams had just reached the southernmost edge of the valley where the KGB had been sighted by the snowmobile units. All teams were now in position to advance, take the fight to the KGB. Blake figured he could take care of the Russians quickly, and with little bloodshed by his own men.

Now, some redneck assholes had decided to play hero.

He had no choice.

They had to be dealt with right away.

"What do you make of this?" Benedict wanted to know.

"I don't know, Captain," Blake growled. He looked up the slope. It was a good two hundred yards' climb to the top. Boulders and jagged rimrock concealed the crest. Fog was an added problem. But one of his teams halfway up the slope had reported sighting a KGB sniper unit. The colonel had ordered them to secure cover and sit tight until further instructions.

Blake looked back at the new arrivals. Arrivals, hell. DOA was what those idiots were going to be shortly. The mist only cloaked the southern half of the lake. Once those men cleared the fog it would be open season on them by KGB snipers.

"Stupid bastards," Blake muttered to himself.

"Sir?" Benedict said.

"Take your team, Captain, and intercept that group in the woods. I'll alert the snowmobile units. They'll move in from behind those people. I don't know who they are, or what the hell they're doing here, and I don't care. Take them by surprise, if possible. I want prisoners. Hell, who knows," he growled, peering back up the slope, "if they're looking to get involved, we just might have some use for them."

Benedict smiled knowingly.

Then, a chopper parted the mist that cloaked the southern wall of rock.

Both Blake and Benedict peered at the whirlybird.

"Take a LAW, Captain," Blake ordered. "If that bird's their fire support, bring it down."

As Benedict moved out with his killteam, the colonel moved up the slope.

The fog swallowed Blake and his three-man death squad.

HE WASN'T SURE where he was.

He wasn't even sure who he was.

He just knew that they meant to kill him.

The four men at the bottom of the slope were camouflaged in white. But that didn't fool him. The man with the strange accent back at the place where he'd been imprisoned had warned him that people were coming to kill him. To kill all of them.

But he had the gun, a big heavy rifle with a funny-shaped magazine. Like a banana, he kept thinking.

But kept hearing instead, Murder. They want to murder you. You must kill them all. Or you will die. You will die! Die! DIE!

He turned, looked back at the faces of those who had been set free with him. They followed him. They stared at him as if waiting for him to give the word to attack. Why? Why did they wait for him? Did they look up to him? Who were they?

Who was he?

Crocker. Lem. That was the only name he could come up with. It was the only name that would stay inside his head.

He was terrified.

The world seemed to rush straight into his eyes. A blazing, blinding maze of twisted color, of sounds screaming through his mind.

Kill. Kill them all!

He rushed the four men at the foot of the slope, holding back on the trigger of his assault rifle. A terrible racket exploded inside of his head. But he didn't care. He had to save himself.

And he was safe as long as he killed them.

Anastas Kosygin and his three-man killteam turned their AKMs toward the charging lunatics.

But it was too late.

Death overtook them with a wave of flashing metal and slashing blades.

14

There had been no time for Kosygin to react to the frenzied attack by the freed inmates of Jarkin asylum. The attention of the KGB assassin and his team had been riveted on the CIA advance. And from the northeast ridges of the valley they had also spotted the Long Knives.

The lunatics seemed to come from out of nowhere. Their blazing guns and hacking blades parted the white swirl behind the Russian squad.

Before the death blows landed, Kosygin experienced a depthless sense of self-hatred. He knew his death was indirectly at his own hand. He had followed orders from his superiors, done their bidding as he had for many years in his service for the KGB.

And he was suddenly very sorry. He was merely an instrument at the disposal of the system. A tool to be bought, honed and used. His life had not been his own. And his death now, too, belonged to someone else.

Kosygin saw the bullets pulverizing his comrades, their whitesuits chewed up into tattered red strips. Then, an incredible fire seared through his legs as a volley of 7.62 mm lead shredded cloth, flesh, shattering the bones in his thighs, knees and shins. He was dying, he knew, as he desperately scrabbled for his AKM.

And there was no hope for him.

Worse still, he was crippled. A man reduced to some bloody, mangled worm, crawling on the ground in a vain attempt to save his life. He found it strange that the taste of death was so bittersweet.

It was useless to resist the end. He was completely at the mercy of the steel that sliced into him from above.

Kosygin tasted his own blood as it sprayed over his face. But the nightmarish reality of his own mutilation became blurred to him in less than a second. Twisted ghouls' faces meshed before his eyes, faded to a warped gray giant puppet figure. The agony of the steel driving through his flesh, grating bone and bursting organs in his chest, vanished. And a strange disembodied numbness swept over him.

Indeed, he longed for death. But it did not come nearly as fast as he wanted.

A prickly sensation ran across his scalp. A voice inside his head told him he should be terrified.

He did not want to live.

But Death suddenly terrified him.

Something told him that he had been sacrificed by his superiors. They, of course, did not care whether he lived or died.

He wondered why.

He wondered just what his life had meant.

Certainly, he thought, there was no meaning in his death. The KGB would win or lose this war with or without him.

He suddenly understood what the Communist machine was all about.

In his death he saw the answer.

Power. Control. Domination.

Life was less than cheap to those who had the power. Within that KGB machine of terror, life, living meant next to nothing.

And he was dying for nothing.

Because he had lived for nothing.

BOLAN SLID OUT onto a twenty-foot ledge overlooking the southern edge of the valley. The chopper was the first thing he saw. A twin-turbine exec Bell job. The fuselage door to the Bell was open and a gunner with a high-powered rifle sat in the opening. Below him, Bolan made out the figures of the Long Knives. Silently, he cursed them for their interference, then for their stupidity. Even though the fog boiled up over the frozen lake like giant white cloud balls, any casual observer from his position could see that only half of the lake was covered by fog.

The Long Knives had come for him, Bolan knew. But what they wanted and what they were about to get were worlds apart.

The Long Knives were walking straight into their own deaths. The Bell, hovering thirty feet above the marching Long Knives, didn't help their luck either. If that was a crack paramilitary team who presented some threat to anybody, Bolan figured he could make short work out of them with a BB gun.

But the ten Long Knives he spotted were only about half of the fanatic right-wing group. Where were the others?

Bolan waited to find the answer.

Within moments that answer came to him in a din of hellscreams and blistering autofire.

THE GROUND BENEATH Joe Lala's feet felt funny. Beneath the virgin snow the surface seemed as hard as rock, and as slick as ice.

Ice! Goddammit, he thought, fighting down a sense of rising panic. He and the others were walking on ice. Lala cleared away a patch of snow with his boot, confirmed his suspicions.

He wondered if Snake had known this. He wondered if the little son of a bitch even cared.

Then he cleared the fog, stared out over another hundred yards of icebed. And where was all this fog he'd been hearing about, anyway? The view to the other side was as clear as daylight. Not even a wisp of mist all the way to the tree- and snow-covered shoreline.

But Lala decided he'd better not show the others any sign of anxiety or indecision. Even though he began to shake like a wet dog beneath his sheepskin coat. But someone did notice.

"Y'awright there, Joe?" Otis Borton asked.

"Yeah, yeah," he growled.

"Cold gettin' to ya?" Borton persisted.

"Naw. Let's shut it up and keep moving, all right?"

Behind Lala the Long Knives spread out.

Lala turned as the helicopter followed the group, the chopper's rotor wash sweeping away the fog. Lala looked up at the door gunner, who waved down at him, and cursed the dumbasses in that bird.

Lala never saw the streaks of flame and smoke overhead. And neither did he see the top of Otis Borton's head explode like a dropped melon.

No, Joe Lala became instantly concerned about saving his own skin as the helicopter directly behind him went up in a roaring fireball.

Lala and the other Long Knives bellyflopped to the snow, covering their heads. Flaming debris pounded the icebed around the Long Knives. Chunks of flaming wreckage seemed to hang suspended, then plunged for the frozen lake.

Lala heard several curses behind him, a shout of panic. Then the slippery ice beneath his hands shuddered violently as the ruined hulk slammed through the icebed.

Jagged sheets of ice knifed up into the air behind the Long Knives.

Water geysered into the air on impact with the downed chopper.

Black smoke clouds boiled over the Long Knives.

Like some grounded behemoth the twisted, fiery chopper hull leaned up out of the water. Flames crackled for several long moments, then sizzled, hissed as the wreckage slid beneath the ice.

Wild-eyed, Lala searched the mist that cloaked the northern slopes. The silence around him became leaden. No one spoke.

Lala listened to the rasping breath of the frightened men around him, glimpsed their plumes of expelled air.

Then the ice sheet groaned like wood around the Long Knives.

Cursing, Lala jumped to his feet, but slipped in his haste and fell.

The groaning turned into one long cracking of ice.

"Don't go back!" Lala yelled at the others. "We gotta make it to the other side."

A Long Knife screamed as the ice around him parted, swallowed him whole into a watery fissure. Lala saw that man vanish from sight.

Then Lala watched as three other Long Knives toppled, their faces mysteriously punched in at the nose. But the blood that masked those agony-contorted faces was no mystery.

Some bastard was sniping at them. Picking them off like rats in a barrel.

Lala bolted. But a bullet found his leg. Lala nosedived to the icebed, the M-16 flying from his hand. Teeth gritted against the fiery waves of pain, he tried to reach out for the M-16.

Half of his hand vanished before his eyes. Howling, he jerked back the bloody stump.

"You goddamned motherfucker!" he screamed.

Lala saw Eddie James running toward him. Good, Lala thought, help.

But a spray of crimson followed the back of Eddie's head across the icebed.

Panic seized Lala. Paralyzed, he saw his fellow Long Knives corkscrewing to the ice.

But the bastards doing the sniping weren't shooting to kill all of them. Why, Lala raged to himself.

The hammering of feet, the weight of thudding bodies on the breaking ice only opened, lengthened the cracks in the surface.

Lala rolled onto his side. He felt the ice weaken beneath him, heard the brittle crack, the horrifying sound of his impending doom. He cried out for help as the ice gave way beneath him like glass. He clawed at the slippery edge, splashing down into the water. Water so cold he turned numb within seconds.

A Long Knife slid to a stop beside Lala.

Twisting his head sideways, he stared for a moment into lifeless eyes. His brother Long Knife's brains leaked out into the snow.

COLONEL THOMAS BLAKE watched as the Long Knives dropped like bowling pins. Screams ripped across that watery grave. But that was all Blake heard at the moment. The Russian assassins had been forced to show a hand. They were using Dragunov sniper rifles fitted with silencers. And Blake didn't have the first goddamn idea where that Russian sniper team was situated.

For the redneck fools on the broken icebed, though, it was all over but the screaming.

Long moments of painful moaning followed sharp cries of agony when Soviet sniper lead found flesh. It didn't puzzle Blake at all as to why the KGB did not just finish this hellish ghoul show. They had created a torture chamber out on that icebed, leaving the survivors wounded and stranded. The KGB was hoping that others would go to the aid of those wounded.

Blake would just as soon let them suffer as die. They had stuck their butts into somebody else's business. And they'd gotten burned. By God, he swore to himself, he would find out who the others were.

If any of those good ol' boy assholes walked away from that valley as his prisoners, then Blake had plans for them.

"They got a fix on those rocket teams," Blake heard his radioman tell him.

"Open up on that position with the LAWs and M-203s," Blake ordered.

The radioman hesitated.

Blake knew what the man was thinking. Flame and smoke from the rocket launchers would give away their own position. Bullshit to that, he said to himself. He had to get those RPG teams.

Or they would all be checking out of the last frontier

BELOKAI WATCHED HIS TARGET splash helplessly in the lake for a moment. Carefully, he lined up his target's bearded face in the cross hairs, drew a steady bead on that visage of terror. A thin smile slashed the assassin's lips. Then he triggered a high-powered round that cracked open the man's forehead like an eggshell.

Joe Lala's head snapped back, his body slapping the water's surface like a board.

Belokai turned his attention to more important matters.

His RPG-7 team was positioned on a shelf, a little more than forty meters west of his current cover. From below his rocket squad, Belokai gave the signal for them to bombard the valley slope with HE rounds.

Then the sky appeared to part in a blinding flash above Belokai. The air sizzled with flame and smoke. A high-explosive detonation rocked the ground beneath Belokai. Dismembered bits and chunks of the four-man RPG-7 team rained down the cliffside. Giant whooshing fireballs vaporized whatever was left of those men.

Belokai, Dmivsky and Chaadeyev covered their heads as hunks of stone pelted them.

Through the ringing in his ears, the Russian colonel managed to make out the faint sounds of return autofire by his men. Rocket flash and smoke had given away the CIA team's position, he knew.

But Belokai would find satisfaction in nothing until every last American was dead. Until he declared decisive victory over the CIA gangsters. Until he claimed the head of Mack Bolan.

Ordering Dmivsky and Chaadeyev to follow, Belokai set out to take the war to his enemies.

THE EXPLOSIVE ROAR of battle swept through the valley, reached the eyes and ears of Mack Bolan. Quickly, he made his way down the southern slope, angling east toward the woods. Big Thunder filled his right hand, and Little Lightning was in his left. All hell had broken loose. For either side it was now free-fire time. Every man was about to become a target.

The sides mattered to Bolan, but he was grimly aware that someone else might not give a damn about whose flag he was fighting under.

The screams of the dead and the dying echoed from the slaughterbed as more Long Knives were drilled into the water by KGB snipers. From what Bolan could see none of those guys was going to make it out of that free-fire zone. Free fire only for the KGB snipers, yeah. Those Long Knives were going to cash in their chips, damn right, but only after the KGB killers had their perverse fun with them.

Because of the distance to the other side of the valley and the thick patches of fog, Bolan was unable to get a clear fix on the CIA-KGB battle zone. But if the CIA was advancing, then the KGB had secured a defensive position along the crest of those hills.

Bolan decided to move northeast, then cut up the slopes, close down on the KGB killteams from their left flank.

He would try his damnedest to stay away from the CIA hit squad and their line of fire.

Suddenly, Bolan glimpsed the snowmobiles as they swept through a wall of fog. He saw the mounted M-60s blazing, the machines rocketing into the woods.

Bolan found a gully, an easier path to the bottom of the slope.

He quickened his strides.

Into the valley of death.

15

It was one bridge that would stay burned.

Death, it seemed to Milt Freeman, had a way of doing that. At the moment he didn't really care how many bridges he burned between himself and his fellow Long Knives. Just as long as he stayed alive.

Still, Freeman couldn't escape the screams, the pleas for help as the dead, the dying and the doomed slid off the broken ice slabs and vanished into the lake. And the two Long Knives who clung to life were finished off within moments. But not until Freeman witnessed their bodies convulsing in agony as silenced lead ripped into their legs and arms. Those tortured men flopped around on the shattered ice sheet like fish out of water. Then headshots spread their brains over the snow and churning red water.

Freeman didn't dare look any of his men in the eye. He sensed they were ready to turn on him. They would never understand that in war lives sometimes had to be sacrificed for the greater good.

Then Freeman detected a faint buzzing sound. He signaled his men to stop, waved an arm for them to spread out.

Freeman scoured the woods, peered at the curling, drifting veils of fog. He saw something move down the slope to the east. But that wasn't the source of the buzzing noise that grew louder by the second.

"Freeze!"

Freeman jolted his attention toward the assault rifles trained on him. The leader of the Long Knives froze.

One of Freeman's boys wasn't so smart. He opened up on Captain Benedict with his M-16. That Long Knife was drilled back into a tree, stitched from crotch to face by 7.62 mm NATO lead. Freeman and the other Long Knives were paralyzed by fear and shock. Death had come to the Long Knives in a lightning flash.

"Okay, okay!" Freeman yelled. He tossed his M-16 to the ground, threw his hands up in the air. "Don't shoot, man! We're all Americans here."

Benedict and his four-man team converged on the radical right-wing mob, closing down on them from their front and flanks. The snowmobiles roared up on the Long Knives from the rear.

Freeman turned his head, watched as the snowmobiles buzzed through the woods. Suddenly, one of the snowmobiles veered toward the slope. The gunner cut loose on something in the fog, the mounted M-60 roaring, spitting flame and heavy lead.

"Don't move," Benedict warned Freeman and the Long Knives.

The second snowmobile raced toward the slope.

Freeman saw the shadow leap out from behind the tree. The driver of the second assault snowmobile didn't see the attacker. Nor the ax. The thud of heavy metal plunging into flesh carried the twelve-yard distance to Benedict and the Long Knives. The unmanned snowmobile streaked away from the inmate. The snowmobile gunner shredded the killer with a long burst from his M-60. A moment later the snowmobile plowed into a tree, a white metal rocket that became instant twisted junk. The next sound that reached the ears of Benedict and the Long Knives was the snap of vertebrae. The impact hurled the gunner from his seat, his head slamming into the tree, his body then spinning away from the tree like a top after the fatal crash.

The other snowmobile raced back toward Benedict.

The CIA paramilitary team gathered the weapons of the Long Knives.

"Hey, look, man," Freeman said. "You guys have made a mistake here."

"Shut up, little man," Benedict rasped. "From here on out you speak only when you're told to."

Freeman restrained his scowl. He felt the eyes of his men crawling all over his backside. He felt their rage and contempt.

Their numbers had been cut in half in less than twenty-four hours. And they were now prisoners.

Stripped of weapons.

Stripped of dignity.

Stripped finally of their belief in themselves as warriors. The evidence of that lay three thousand miles back in West Virginia. And more evidence bobbed in the murky, crimson waters of the lake.

Milt Freeman suddenly realized he had done more than just burn a few bridges.

He had kicked his own ass.

But, he vowed to himself, he wasn't going down with the ship.

FROM THE HIGH GROUND, Bolan had seen the capture of the Long Knives by the CIA killteam. He had also witnessed the murderous attack on the snowmobile unit by the freed inmates.

Swiftly Bolan moved through the woods, angling northeast up the slope.

A bloodcurdling scream ripped the air.

Whirling, the Executioner hosed the wild-eyed lunatic with a Little Lightning burst. The man tumbled down the slope, the meat cleaver flying from his hand, banging off a rock.

From the crest of the slope two more zombies stepped through the fog, AKMs blazing. Big Thunder bucked twice in the Executioner's right fist, 240-grain chest-tunnelers kicking both lunatics out of Bolan's sight, flinging them over the other side of the rise.

Anxious thoughts about Grimaldi's safety passed through Bolan's mind. There was no telling now what his friend might find with deeper recon of the zone.

Combat senses on full alert, Bolan quickly climbed the slope. Topping the rise, he crouched behind a boulder. A large band of lunatics marched across the snowfield to the east. Toting Russian hardware or sharp lethal weapons, that mob headed south toward Taskinoma.

Bolan knew he had to end one war right away in order to get to another. Knowledge of the KGB master list was with Baknov and Kelly. Bolan wanted that intel.

And if the lunatics made it to the town of Taskinoma they could very well turn that remote frontier outpost into a slaughterbed.

Bolan hustled along the crest of the rise. Several hundred yards north the eastern spine of the mountain range waited for the Executioner's assault.

Lev Belokai froze.

There was no mistaking the familiar rolling thunder.

He had heard it back in West Virginia.

Where Bolan the Executioner had made known his presence of death.

Belokai and his two-man team of Dmivsky and Chaadeyev were now making their way to the higher ground north of the valley. Two miles north, perched on the edge of the cliff, loomed the cabin.

That was Belokai's destination. That was where he would finish his war against the CIA paramilitary force.

But now, without ample rocket-fire support, he knew the risks were greater. The CIA would advance up the slope. They would believe they had turned the tide of battle, that they had the KGB on the run. Retreat by his forces would signal the CIA that they were on the verge of victory.

But it was a false alarm he had sounded, Belokai knew. He had thrown up a smoke screen. Shortly the black siren would wail.

Belokai had sent two fireteams to engage the CIA criminals. Those two fireteams might not survive against the greater numbers and the heavier firepower that the CIA criminals had shown. But the Russian knew his men would inflict casualties on the Americans. And a firefight in his wake, in the KGB's apparent retreat, would give him sufficient time to hunt down and kill Mack Bolan.

A sudden noise startled Belokai. He spun, ready to rip to pieces anything that moved with his RPK-74.

Instead of living human flesh, what he found were three caribou. They stood, large, brown-skinned, antlered statues.

Silently, Belokai chastised himself for his edginess. It was Bolan, he thought. His nerves were frayed dangerously thin by his burning desire to strike the feared Executioner dead.

Belokai glimpsed Dmivsky and Chaadeyev.

Dmivsky chuckled nervously.

The caribou turned away from the Russians and bolted.

Belokai stitched the hides of the caribou with a long RPK fusillade. A rain of 5.45 mm lead hammered the animals to the ground, fur and blood washing over the snow.

Dmivsky stopped chuckling.

Belokai turned away from the twitching carcasses, brushed past the hesitant Dmivsky and Chaadeyev, growled, "Move, comrades."

Dmivsky and Chaadeyev fell in behind Belokai. With haste, they followed the KGB's master assassin.

IF THERE WAS A WAR raging between the CIA kill-squad and their KGB counterparts, Special Operative James Kelly wasn't aware of it. In fact, at the moment he didn't even really care to know about that war. He was far removed from the zone. And his mind was even farther removed from reality.

Kelly was now working on his second bottle of Cutty Sark. Straight up. If he didn't despise the Russian potato faces so much he would have bought a round for his drinking comrade, Baknov. The Soviet defector was no lightweight when it came to big-league Scotch whiskey. Baknov wasn't much for conversation, but Kelly was in no mood to talk. One thing and one thing only had momentarily bridged the gap between communism and capitalism. It was called feeling good on a belly full of liquor. And the world be damned.

Kelly drew deep on his unfiltered Camel. When a man could go through two packs of butts in two hours, the agent thought, he knew he had a small problem with nicotine. When the harsh smoke no longer bit at his throat and lungs and the phlegm he hacked up had a rather pleasant taste to it he knew he had somehow turned one deadly vice into one of life's perverse but finer pleasures.

But when Kelly began to fancy himself as the Messiah of CIA covert operations, he knew he wasn't drinking enough. Sure, he'd won several Distinguished Intelligence Crosses and medals and stars. And he'd performed feats under fire, heroics that were nothing short of miracles, during sensitive operations in hotspots that few operatives would touch without the hand of God gracing their shoulders. He'd taken plenty of heat from superiors when some other fuck-head in the field should have gone down the toilet.

Kelly took another drag on his Camel, sucked down another shot. He looked around the crowded, smoky room. If he didn't know better he would have sworn he was in Fort Lauderdale at spring break. Dozens of laughing, wild-eyed women, all of them hungry for quick sex and easy money.

And there was enough fur in the saloon to outfit a Cossack army.

But best of all, there seemed to be an endless supply of liquor. The beer never stopped flowing from about ten kegs behind the two bars. If he could have gotten rid of the noise, Kelly would have considered instant and permanent retirement in Taskinoma. But the billiard balls never ceased to clack on the three tables at the far end of the room. And the jukebox blared on continuously with an assortment of country and rock and roll headaches.

The saloon's interior decorator, he thought, definitely had an animal fetish. Stuffed animal heads on walnut plaques lined every wall. Grizzly. Caribou. Bighorn sheep. Wolf.

And the way several of the uglier faces in that saloon were looking in the direction of him and his Russian comrade, Kelly got a gut feeling that some taxidermist had just been called in from the cold.

Kelly was in no mood or shape to slug it out with any miner, pipeline worker, trapper or anybody else in the barroom at the moment. What he wanted more than anything else right then was the little Eskimo number sitting at a table at the far end of the bar.

Kelly looked at Baknov. The defector was strung out, the SOD man knew, and the physical and mental wear and tear of weeks of interrogation showed on Baknov's face. The Soviet had appeared to age ten years in just a few weeks under the Company's thumb. But Kelly had the gut instinct that Baknov was bona fide. The CIA had had agents working on Baknov years before the Soviet defected from the KGB's London desk.

Now, a ghost from the Company's past wanted the defector all for himself. Mack Bolan. A one-man army crusade cleansing the world of the scourge of global terrorism. Kelly wasn't so sure he shouldn't just hand the damned guy over to Bolan. No matter which way the CIA-KGB war here turned out. Perhaps Bolan was right. One good man could do a whole lot more to inflict damage on the KGB than an entire organization. Particularly an organization that was handcuffed by the bleeding hearts and the do-gooders.

One man, dammit.

Suddenly Kelly wasn't in a mood to drink anymore.

16

Jack Grimaldi broke through a patch of fog and brought the chopper in low as he soared across the snowfield. Two hundred yards ahead he saw Jarkin Institute. There was no sign of life.

Within moments, though, Bolan's ace pilot discovered plenty of signs of death. Perhaps a dozen bodies littered the courtyard as Grimaldi set the aircraft down just inside the battered front gates. Knives and meat cleavers were strewed around the corpses.

Shutting the Bell down, Grimaldi fisted his M-16. Two bodies were wedged between the doorjamb and the doors to the front entrance of the asylum. Something warned Grimaldi that he would find a massacre beyond those doors.

A lump the size of a grapefruit lodging in his belly, Grimaldi opened the cockpit door and stepped out onto the compound. He had been through enough wars with the Executioner to sense the threat of an unseen, dangerous presence. That presence was now somewhere nearby, perhaps watching, stalking him.

Judging by the looks of murderous rage frozen on their faces and the knives still clutched in their hands,

Grimaldi believed that the dead in the courtyard had turned their weapons on one another.

Quickly, the pilot climbed the front steps. He peered through the crack in the doorway, the stench of death cloying in his nostrils. Then he saw the bullet-shredded bodies of the Jarkin staff slumped along the base of the wall. Blood bathed the walls and the floor.

The place was a slaughterhouse.

Grimaldi listened to the silence, straining his ears to pick up any sound. Nothing.

He pushed the door open, stepped over the dead, moved into the foyer. What he saw was senseless butchery. Someone had lined the Jarkin staff up against the wall and executed them like sick cattle.

Back braced against the wall opposite the carnage, Grimaldi peered around the corner. And what he saw twisted his guts.

Kneeling over the body of a dead guard, two female inmates were cannibalizing the corpse. Their faces were wet with blood.

Fighting down the bile, Grimaldi carefully stepped out into the hallway.

The cannibals were unaware of the lone man.

The M-16 began to lower by Grimaldi's side as his mind tried to register the enormity of what had happened at the asylum.

Suddenly he sensed movement from behind. He whirled and glimpsed the gleaming head of an ax as it craned to split open his face. With adrenaline surging like wildfire through his veins, the pilot reacted instantly, throwing himself into the wall, away from the razor-sharp edge of the ax. He hit the wall, the sudden impact punching the air from his lungs. He dodged the death strike but the ax grazed his shoulder. Instant white-hot pain blazed the length of Grimaldi's arm as the edge of the heavy blade nicked flesh.

The wild-eyed lunatic didn't give his intended victim a chance to recover. Screaming, the crazy pivoted, drove the blade toward Grimaldi's head. Ducking the potentially decapitating blow, Grimaldi felt the air swish over his scalp before he heard the ax thud into the wall.

Grimaldi had unknowingly stepped right into the bowels of hell. And he knew there was only one way he would get out.

Before the axman could pull the weapon free of the broken plaster, Grimaldi rammed his M-16's muzzle into the madman and squeezed the trigger.

The target jerked back from the blazing M-16, staggered like a drunk.

For a second, Grimaldi watched, incredulous. The gut-shredding M-16 rounds didn't even seem to faze the lunatic. Grimaldi stitched that mask of mindless rage as the madman charged him, lifting the ax. This time, the lunatic went down and stayed down.

A bloodcurdling shriek ripped through the hallway. Spinning, Grimaldi triggered his M-16, drilled one of the cannibals back into the wall. The woman's meat cleaver clattered to the floor. Grimaldi's 5.56 mm fusillade erased her face forever.

Then Grimaldi turned the assault rifle on the other cannibal, hammered her into the ravaged remains of her gruesome meal.

The killshots echoed down the long corridor.

Grimaldi checked his shoulder wound. Blood flowed freely from the gash. It would require a good cleaning, possibly some stitches to close the wound. But the first-aid kit was back in the chopper. And Grimaldi decided the wound could wait.

The Stony Man pilot made a quick search of the building for any survivors. He found nothing but more hacked-up, dismembered bodies of lunatics who'd turned weapons on one another. Windows had been shattered. Doors splintered. Broken bottles and glass littered medicine cabinets. Stuffing covered the seats of cushions slashed open.

The signs of minds gone mad were everywhere.

As Grimaldi stepped out of the ward and into the main corridor, autofire blistered at him from the main foyer. Lead sizzlers chewed up the doorframe as he jerked back for cover.

Howling laughter competed with the roar of the AK-47. Autofire kept Grimaldi pinned behind the doorway for several moments.

Then the Kalashnikov's magazine emptied on the lunatic. The crazed-sounding laughter washed over the ace flier's position with eerie clarity.

Spinning out of the doorway, he unleashed his M-16, kicked the laughing madman off his feet with a sustained burst.

As Grimaldi moved up the corridor, he wished for eyes in the back of his head. Insanity could come at him from anywhere, at any second. He turned, covering his rear, checking all doorways.

Even as he neared death, the lunatic managed a fit of strange barking laughter. Blood bubbled over his twitching lips. He writhed on the floor like a man under electric shock.

Grimaldi finished the crazy with a mercy round.

The stench of death and blood became overpowering to Grimaldi the longer he stayed in that charnel house.

Quickly, Jack Grimaldi left the asylum.

With the lunatic mob on the prowl in their mindless lust for flesh and blood, there was no telling what would happen in the CIA-KGB war on the slopes of the Alaska Range.

Grimaldi raced toward the chopper.

He was sure Mack Bolan would need him now. Perhaps, he thought, more than ever.

SILENCED BERETTA 93-R in hand, the Executioner stalked the four-man KGB killteam. He figured they were less than a dozen yards ahead of him now, moving west through the woods. He saw a clearing beyond the woods that led to higher ground, which appeared to be the KGB execution squad's immediate destination.

The way the team hustled through the woods, Bolan believed they were closing in on the CIA paramilitary force. An ambush most likely.

Bolan decided to take the numbers as they fell.

He would have to.

The wild cards were stacking up.

The unit spread out as they advanced. Bolan watched the KGB goon guarding the team's left flank. Every dozen yards or so the sentry would turn, check the team's rear.

Bolan waited until the savage turned again, then took him out with a silenced 9 mm round.

The kill alerted the other three Russian hit men a second later.

But the Executioner had lined up his gun sights on another target in the blink of an eye, eliminating a second KGB gunman. Another quick chug from the Beretta bored through the third Soviet butcher's eye.

A short burst of autofire blazed from the last KGB thug's AKM. Bullets drilled into the snow in front of Bolan as he dropped that goon with a headshot.

The Executioner didn't have to worry about the autofire alerting any troop movement ahead.

From the distance came the rumble of detonating frag grenades, the screams of the wounded and the dying.

Bolan drew Big Thunder.

STEVHKIN'S F1 GRENADE landed in front of the snowmobile as it streaked through the woods and bore down on Kovekny's five-man killsquad to the north. The M-60 mounted on the back of the machine blazed for a second in an attempt to break free the three-man CIA team that was wedged in a Soviet cross fire.

Stevhkin saw one of his comrades take a head hit.

A millisecond later the grenade detonated. Bits and pieces of the snowmobile razored through the woods, banged off trees as the blast flipped the shredded wreckage up and over in a backward somersault. The two Americans in that snowmobile came down on their heads. But Stevhkin knew that the concussion had already killed them.

Now there was no place for the CIA squad to run or hide. For the past hour Stevhkin and his team had followed the Americans, alerting Kovekny of the operatives' every movement.

The American fools blundered into the trap like blind men. Just as Stevhkin had hoped.

And now they paid the price for their error. In blood.

Waves of ComBloc lead sizzlers washed over the Company men's position. The Americans fired in blind panic, spinning in every direction in a desperate attempt to return the deadly Soviet fire. But a scissoring hurricane of AKM and RPK rounds found the CIA force within seconds. Tree bark mingled with flesh, blood and cloth, dozens of ragged red holes blossoming over the bodies of the Americans.

The salvo of killshots was indeed extended, but not unnecessary, Stevhkin knew. The pulverized bodies would serve as a message for anyone who would later stumble over the carnage.

Victory, Stevhkin thought, was going to be every bit as sweet and glorious as Kovekny and Colonel Belokai had promised.

Stevhkin couldn't wait to return to Moscow.

"So, YOU THOUGHT you'd come here and play soldier boy, is that right?" Colonel Thomas Blake growled at Milt Freeman.

For a long moment the colonel looked at the leader of the Long Knives in disgust. Both Blake's and Benedict's fireteams were now gathered in the gully halfway up the slope. Blake looked toward the crest. Beyond the rise stretched a plain, another wooded area that led to higher ground. The cabin where the American traitors were was at the top of that high ground, the zone of their final assault.

The Long Knives had been stripped of their weapons, and Blake was pondering over what use he could put the ragtag band of hillbilly soldiers to.

"Well, Little Napoleon," Blake continued, "you're going to get that chance."

Freeman looked anxious. It was obvious he didn't like the ominous ring to Blake's words.

"Hey, look, Colonel," Freeman implored, "we're all Americans here, right? There's a common enemy we're fighting here, right? Why don't you give us back our weapons, man? We could be some help to you, I know it.''

Blake showed Freeman a twisted smile. The colonel turned his head, looked back at the shattered icebed. There, several bodies floated on the lake's surface.

"You mean help like that?" Blake asked.

Freeman's gaze faltered. Anger, fear masked the faces of the other Long Knives behind Freeman.

"That was a mistake," Freeman explained.

"No kidding," the colonel growled. "No, *your* mistake was coming here and trying to butt yourselves into something that's way too hot for a bunch of weekend warriors from hicktown U.S.A."

Anger flared in Freeman's eyes. "Yeah, Colonel, well if you CIA dudes are so fuckin' bad, how come my weekend warriors capped those spooks back in West Virginia?"

Blake admitted to himself that he had to wonder about that, too. He thought about the wild card that had blazed a trail of carnage through the Company smoke screen.

"Apparently those same hardmen you sent got capped themselves, little man," Blake said. "What do you know about that?"

Freeman snorted. "All I know is I want the bastard that did it. That's why we came here. Not to walk right into the guns of your stinking war. I want to kill the dude who snuffed out my people right under my own nose. When I see that bastard again . . .''

"So, you've seen him?"

"Yeah, I've seen him. But it was dark when he hit our place and I didn't get a good look. We were holding his pilot, and the dude came for him. The pilot was the one who told us about this war here with the KGB."

Captain Benedict turned a puzzled look on Blake. "What the hell? Nobody outside of the division knew about this."

Freeman chuckled. "Well, somebody sure as hell did. And if they weren't CIA, then I'd say you boys got another problem on your hands. 'Cause that dude who hit us was one big, bad son of a bitch. And I'd bet anything he's somewhere out here right now. Maybe even watching you, Colonel. Maybe he's waiting for you to make the big move. Then he'll just zero in on the KGB himself." Freeman chuckled again. "And all you big free-lancin' ex-Government Issues go back to Washington with a whole lot of egg on your face. I've got visions of I-ran dancing in my head."

"Shut up, little man," Blake softly snarled. "You talk like that again, one of my guys who just happened to be there might put another hole in your head.

"Now, you listen to me, all of you," he growled at the rest of the Long Knives. "The way I'm reading this is you came here to ice the guy that wasted some of your numbers. I don't know who this guy is, but if he's here, he'll show himself sooner or later. And when he does, he's mine. We're holding the guns, which makes you my prisoners. Any heroes here will be dead ones.

Now, I'm going to assume this, uh, guy that you want so bad, shares some of the responsibility for the hit on the dummy safehouse. I'm also assuming he wants a piece of this action, reasons unknown.

"You Long Knives got burned. But for you people, the worst may be yet to come. And from here on, if you don't follow my orders to the letter I'll kill every one of you where you stand. I won't say a word. I'll just pull the trigger."

Blake paused to let the warning sink in. Freeman and the Long Knives stood in hard silence.

"Order all units to advance," the Colonel told his radioman. "We're going in to finish it. I want that cabin taken within the hour. Let's move it, Shorty," he ordered Freeman, stepping aside, gesturing with his M-16 for Freeman to move past him. "You and your boys can walk point. This is your big chance."

Big chance, Blake knew, meant this punk and his Long Knives were dead meat. The slaughter on the lake had shown the colonel just how he could put the Long Knives to use.

And use them was exactly what he planned to do.

For a time they slogged along in silence. They reached the crest of the slope.

Freeman hesitated. He stared out across a forty-yard stretch of open ground. Ahead was the trail and at the top of that was the cabin.

Colonel Blake jammed the muzzle of his M-16 against Freeman's back. "Move it!" he rasped.

"What if they're—" Freeman started to protest.

"What if they are?" Blake shot back.

Freeman muttered an oath. He was being played as bait for the KGB. A real sucker, he thought bitterly. Invisible assassins, he feared, were all over the slope that led to the cabin. Suddenly, Milt Freeman felt weak, shamed. He had lost all face with his men. He was trapped in a nightmare. And the only escape was quite possibly his own death.

Colonel Blake's ten-man team spread out along the crest, dropped down into prone positions. The soldiers guarding the CIA men's flanks positioned themselves so that they also covered the rear. A little more than one hundred yards east the remaining CIA unit moved up the slope. The one-and-a-half-ton transport truck and the twin-turbine chopper that Belokai had commandeered were parked a dozen yards west of Blake's position.

"You're a fucking bastard, you know that, Colonel," Freeman snarled.

"Yeah, ain't life beautiful?" Blake replied, shoving Freeman in the back. "What the hell's going on with fireteam B?" he asked his radioman.

"I can't raise contact, sir."

Blake cursed. "The sons of bitches got them. Christ! Tell fireteam A to make sure they cover our rear from the east."

"Yes, sir," the radioman affirmed.

The Long Knives took several tentative steps across the open ground.

"Get the lead out, mister!" Blake snarled at Freeman.

Snake Eyes Freeman turned a look of depthless hatred on Blake. He had never wanted to kill a man more in his life. No, he decided, killing the CIA bastard outright would be too good for him. He wanted to see Blake suffer, squirm, plead for his life. Freeman knew Blake would get his. Snake Eyes only hoped he was around to see it.

Then a piercing shriek knifed the air.

One of the Long Knives crumpled to the snow.

Everyone stood stock-still. All eyes turned on the Long Knife writhing around in the snow. The man clutched at his lower leg. Huge steel jaws had snapped that leg nearly in half. Blood, squirted in red jets from the severed arteries in the Long Knife's leg, sprayed across the snow.

The throb of rotor blades echoed across the sky.

Blake looked east. There, a chopper soared over the jumbled ridges.

A tight smile slit Freeman's lips for a second. Then, the leader of the Long Knives bolted across the clearing.

The chopper belonged to the Long Knives.

The sniper in the helicopter's doorway opened up on the CIA squad.

17

The big high-powered Dragunov bucked in Belokai's hands. Through the scope's cross hairs he saw his round strike flesh, shear off a chunk of thigh. The American thug in the KGB assassin's gun sights thrashed in agony, his screams shrill in the cold mountain air. Then, Belokai saw another Long Knife topple to the snow as one of the massive bear traps snapped onto his leg like the jaws of some great predator.

At the moment, Belokai was too enthralled by the horrible punishment he inflicted on the trapped Long Knives to be aware of the throb of the chopper's rotors. Dmivsky had to alert the colonel to the chopper as it swooped toward the killzone.

Then something else caught Belokai's eye. Scouring the killzone, he spotted a lone figure skirting the precipice of a ledge two hundred feet below him. Belokai glimpsed the stainless steel pistol in the man's fist.

Bolan!

He was certain.

But the figure in whitesuit hugged the inner wall of the rock face, and Belokai lost sight of him. The KGB colonel decided to take the hunt to the hunter.

Chaadeyev pointed toward the three-man CIA team as it moved up the eastern slope. "Look."

Belokai looked, all right. But his mind was on the lone figure who had momentarily vanished from his sight.

The motherland urged Belokai on, calling him to glory. His war.

His glory.

Belokai hooked his arm through the Dragunov, picked up his RPK-74.

"Move!" he ordered Dmivsky and Chaadeyev.

As THE CHOPPER HOVERED near the killzone, the door gunman fired wildly at Blake's team.

"Blow it!" the colonel yelled as rotor wash swept snow over his soldiers in a swirling, blinding mist.

Without hesitation, three of the paramilitary operatives turned their M-16s skyward. A trio of 40 mm grenades belched from the M-203s attached to their assault rifles.

Freeman stumbled, pitched to the ground. The Long Knife leader turned his head in time to see his last hope disintegrate in a deafening explosion. A roiling fireball cloud blazed across the sky, vaporizing the aircraft.

"Follow their tracks!" Blake ordered, charging across the open ground as flaming debris plunged to the slope.

Blake raked the ground behind the fleeing Long Knives. "Halt!"

The Long Knives stopped.

Suddenly a four-man KGB team leaped out of the transport truck's bed, AK-47s roaring in their hands. Three of Blake's men closest to that truck bit the bloody snow. As ComBloc lead sizzled the air, Blake's forces reacted instantly to the murderous new threat.

Whirling toward the truck, the CIA hit-squad unleashed a fusillade. Glass shattered under their onslaught, and 7.62 mm slugs peppered the canvas cover.

Blake, Benedict and the surviving six operatives of their squad triggered their M-16s for a long moment, repelling the surprise KGB attack. Soviets jerked, spun, collided under the relentless stream of NATO rounds.

Blake crossed the clearing. Furious, the colonel ran Freeman down. As the biker leader struggled to stand, Blake belted Freeman across the jaw with the butt of his M-16, then rammed the muzzle under Freeman's chin. "Don't try something like that again!" Blake rasped.

"All right, all right," Weeb Jordan said contritely, thrusting his hands high. "Don't shoot. We panicked, man, awright?"

Blake hauled Freeman to his feet.

Flames crackled along the slope, consumed the black hull of the downed chopper. Oily clouds of smoke drifted into the sky.

Agonized cries from the two Long Knives caught in the bear traps sounded loud and shrill following the firefight.

Blake turned, put those two Long Knives out of their misery with an M-16 burst.

"Move it up the trail," Blake ordered Freeman. "Single file."

"You're nuts, Colonel," Freeman said, his stare wide as if he was suddenly trying to comprehend this madness. "You're gonna kill everybody here just to nail the KGB."

"Wrong, little man," Blake growled. "I'm going to kill all of you only if you don't move it. Now."

Freeman hesitated. But the sound of fresh 30-round magazines being slapped into the M-16s seemed to jar Freeman out of his trance.

As Blake's team fanned out into the woods, Freeman and Jordan began to lead the surviving Long Knives up the trail.

"Goddamn you, Freeman," Jordan grumbled, trudging beside his leader. "Goddamn you to hell for this. We're all going to die, you lousy little fuck."

"Shut up," Freeman snarled.

"Silence, both of you," Blake warned, sliding deeper into the cover of the woods. "Or I'll shut you up for good."

"What the hell we s'pposed to do when we reach the top?" Freeman wanted to know.

"You go inside that cabin. If you find two Americans there you free them and wait for us to make it to the top."

"What if they're not there?" Freeman growled.

"You'd just better hope they are."

CROUCHED BEHIND A BOULDER on the ledge overlooking the trail, Bolan had assessed the battle ahead. The KGB had obviously given their CIA counterparts a clear pathway to the mountain trail.

But the Russians had booby-trapped the open ground with bear traps. At the moment, the KGB had made themselves invisible.

Something felt very wrong to Bolan. Gut instinct told the Executioner that the battle's climax was about to take place on the slope leading to the cabin. Gut instinct also warned Bolan that the KGB was about to spring some surprise on the remainder of the CIA and Long Knife forces.

Bolan watched as Colonel Blake threatened Freeman with his M-16. The crackling tongues of fire that lapped up the debris of the Long Knives' chopper obscured Blake's angry words to the Long Knives up the trail.

Bolan opted to clear the ledge, angle up the slope and head off whatever enemy numbers might converge on the Americans.

Then sudden movement to his left alerted him.

Bolan swung the .44 AutoMag in the direction of the three-man CIA team as it skirted the crest of the slope.

They didn't see the Executioner.

But Bolan spotted the frag grenade as it sailed over his head, flying down toward the Americans.

"Grenade!" Bolan shouted at the unsuspecting Company specialists.

Frantic eyes searched for the voice among the rocks. A millisecond later the frag blast ripped through the squad, shredding them across the open ground.

Bolan lunged over the edge of the rock wall. He made out three figures as they scurried down the rocky hillside.

Big Thunder bucked in the Executioner's fist.

One man's head erupted as 240 grains of thunder, muzzling at 1640 feet per second, exploded through his forehead.

Bolan swung his aim instantly, but RPK autofire drove him for cover beneath the lip of the wall. Slugs whined off the rock like frenzied hornets as the Executioner glided down the ledge.

Bolan rose above the edge, drew a bead on his next KGB target. Out of the corner of his eye, Bolan glimpsed the frag grenade as it hurtled toward his position. He triggered a quick round, saw his target double over.

Then the sky seemed to fall on Bolan's head.

There was no defending himself against the frag bomb.

Bolan vaulted off the ledge.

A roaring explosion followed him through the air. Shock waves hammered the Executioner as he plummeted toward the trail. Chunks of stone pelted his skull and his ears rang with the deafening echo of the concussive blast. He saw the trail rushing up at his face. He hit the ground hard, instinctively throwing himself into a roll. But the twenty-foot drop jarred him, drove the air from his lungs. A terrible roar filled his ears, seemed to split his brain in two. For what seemed like an eternity he couldn't move, stunned by the blast.

The sky swam in Bolan's sight.

He willed himself to stay awake. If he fell unconscious now, he knew he was dead.

Then he glimpsed a figure moving along the ledge.

Dead, yeah, he thought. For damn sure. One of the KGB bastards was coming down for him.

Bolan slid his hand beneath the snow, feeling around for Big Thunder. A part of his mind told him that he had other weapons, to reach for the Beretta or the mini-Uzi. Another part of his mind demanded unconsciousness.

With all the willpower that had seen him through countless deadly encounters on the edge of hell, Bolan struggled to keep from going under. Still, his vision blurred, his mind fading in and out. The crackle of the flaming chopper wreckage sounded as if it was miles away.

Bolan drew a deep breath through his nose, the cold air slicing through his reeling senses.

Then he felt his hand touch something. But it wasn't the Automag. He wasn't sure what it was he grasped.

As Bolan struggled to see through the black veil that clouded his vision, Belokai jumped off the ledge. A death's head grimace masked the KGB assassin's features.

Belokai savored his moment of triumph. All those from the motherland who had gone up against the feared and hated Executioner before, and failed, would now be avenged, he thought. The name of Colonel Belokai, master assassin, slayer of the Executioner, would live on forever.

The KGB killer walked toward Bolan.

Bolan rolled onto his side, his arms buried beneath the snow. There was a glazed, faraway look in his eyes. Through the roar in his ears, he heard his mind telling him to wait. To wait for the enemy to show his weakness.

Belokai stopped several feet short of Bolan and looked down at him.

"You are a pitiful sight, Executioner, in your moment of death."

Arrogance? Was that the weakness of the KGB assassin? Bolan wondered.

Belokai took a step forward. Suddenly the toe of his boot caught on a heavy chain link. A look of stunned surprise flashed across his face, quickly gone. In his haste to kill Bolan, he had almost walked into one of the bear traps planted by his comrades.

Silently he cursed himself for the lapse. Then he reached inside his coat to draw the Kukri.

Yes, arrogance was the fatal flaw that would betray the KGB killer, Bolan thought. With his RPK-74 strapped to his shoulder, Belokai had reached for the Kukri with all the certainty of a man assured of victory.

Still waiting, Bolan willed strength into his limbs, watching, feigning helplessness.

Belokai drew the Kukri.

"Do svidaniya," he said, his eyes blazing with vengeance. "Your life belongs to me now, Executioner."

Lifting his leg to avoid the bear trap, the KGB assassin raised the knife high above his head.

With a viselike grip on the flange of the bear trap, Bolan sprang up onto his knees, hurling the deadly steel jaws straight at Belokai's uplifted boot. Belokai's foot struck the pan, released the spring.

The jaws clamped down on Belokai's leg. It took a split second for the shock of the sudden attack to register on the Russian's face.

Then a scream of agony ripped from Belokai's throat, an animallike howl that seemed to be the only sound in the whole universe at that moment.

THE SCREAM SENT A CHILL down Kovekny's spine. It came from somewhere back down the slope behind Kovekny.

The twenty-three-man Russian squad froze, crouched behind a line of trees. Every man turned his head, anxious expressions turned toward the downhill gloom of the wooded slope.

The scream lingered, echoed. It was a sound of unmistakable, excruciating pain.

Who, Kovekny wondered, then forced himself to turn his attention back to the war at hand.

The other Soviets looked to Kovekny for a signal.

Kovekny gave that signal for the team to split up. The CIA, he knew, were now halfway up the slope, closing down on the cabin. Kovekny had to be there to witness his moment of victory.

Stevhkin took half of the force with him. That kill-team angled up the slope, in a direction away from the CIA force.

In case something went wrong at the cabin, Kovekny wanted to surround the Americans, annihilate them with one final ambush.

One final crushing blow.

That was all he needed.

And victory would be his.

THE KUKRI SLIPPED from Belokai's hand. The KGB killer toppled to the snow, blood gushing from his mangled leg.

Bolan sucked in the cold air. The ringing in his ears, the numb sensation in his arms and legs faded. His only thought now was to kill Belokai.

Belokai, the KGB butcher, the heartless killing machine programmed by a terrorist regime that wanted to dominate the world.

Belokai was a cannibal.

Bolan had a one-way ticket for the cannibal.

And he was going to punch that ticket.

A desperate rasping sound rattled around in the assassin's mouth as he clawed at the snow, searching for the Kukri.

Bolan stood, wobbled for a moment on rubbery legs.

Belokai clutched the Kukri, rolled onto his side, the blade arcing up toward Bolan's gut. The Executioner lashed out with a kick, the toe of his boot impacting solidly with Belokai's wrist. Bone shattered. The fighting knife flew from the killer's grasp.

Bolan's fist pistoned down, hammered off Belokai's jaw. For a moment, the Executioner stood over the KGB hit man.

Bolan turned and made a quick search of the immediate area. He spotted the muzzle of Big Thunder protruding out of the snow. As Bolan retrieved the AutoMag, Belokai suddenly seemed to remember he carried the RPK-74.

Bolan plucked the AutoMag out of the snow. Turning back to the KGB killer, he saw Belokai fumbling to unsling the RPK.

The Executioner moved one step toward him. Looming over the KGB master assassin, Bolan lifted the stainless-steel hand cannon, sighted down the 6.5 inch barrel.

A face that had stared down more than one victim during a lifetime of terror, murder and sabotage, looked back at him.

Soulless eyes, the Executioner knew, that had seen more than one innocent life fall prey to his hand.

A sudden, livid hatred twisted Belokai's face. He wrestled the RPK-74 off his shoulder.

Bolan waited. Was that a glimmer of hope he saw in the killer's eyes?

The AutoMag roared in Bolan's fist.

The black dice rolled over the KGB's master assassin.

And Belokai crapped out.

The peals of death trailed off into the vast wilderness.

Bolan took the RPK-74. Using the stock of the heavy machine gun like a cane, the Executioner raked the ground in front of him, searching for any more bear traps as he made his way back to the wall of rock.

A stone clattered off the ledge.

Bolan looked up.

Chaadeyev teetered along the lip of the precipice. Bolan's .44 round had tunneled through the Soviet's stomach.

Bolan raised the AutoMag. But there was no need.

The muzzle of Chaadeyev's AKM wavered, dropped away from Bolan. The Soviet swayed, then fell forward, ramrod stiff.

Bolan heard a crack as the Russian's head slammed off the ledge. The corpse plunged straight toward Bolan, finally thudded to the snow beside the Executioner.

For a moment, Bolan stared down into the lifeless eyes of another face of hell.

Then, Big Thunder in hand, the Executioner moved along the base of the rock wall.

To close those gates of Hell on the KGB.

For now.

For today.

Tomorrow would bring another war, he knew. And the gates of hell would open again.

But the war on the last frontier wasn't over. Yet.

The black dice were still rolling.

18

Milt Freeman would've sworn it was the longest twenty-four hours of his life.

If he had been a man who believed in fate, then he would have believed that he and the Long Knives had somehow been led to this hellzone at the end of the world by forces beyond their control.

At the moment, Freeman decided, his life was definitely out of his control. And it wasn't worth squat.

Freeman turned. Behind him, strung out in a zig-zag line, his men trudged up the trail. His men, he thought bitterly. There was nothing between them now but pure hate. And he couldn't hold those stares of vengeance. If Blake or the KGB didn't get him, then Freeman was sure his own men would melt him.

Freeman searched the woods off to the side of the trail, but he found no sign of Blake, not even a tell-tale cloud of expelled breath coming from behind a tree. But he knew that the CIA team was somewhere in the gloomy depths of the woods.

Then Freeman heard the bone-chilling scream.

Crumpling to the trail, a Long Knife clawed at the razor-sharp steel teeth that had bitten through his leg.

Freeman froze. A look of cold fear showed in his eyes. He had just missed stepping into that bear trap by inches. And his fear edged toward terror, because he was walking point.

Freeman didn't get a chance to linger on the trail or his sudden paranoia. And he discovered exactly where Blake was positioned.

As a Long Knife moved to help his fallen comrade, lead tumblers danced along the snow. Bullets tore into the wounded Long Knife, silenced his screams.

Freeman cursed, hustling away from the line of tracking fire. Panting, he scuffled his feet, kicking the ground ahead in a desperate search for any more bear traps. He heard Weeb Jordan cursing viciously behind him. He wasn't exactly sure who or what Weebie was cursing.

Bullets ricocheted off the rock above Freeman's head.

The leader of the Long Knives scrambled up the trail toward the cabin. Away from the hellfire din behind him.

Freeman longed for this day to come to an end.

BOLAN LISTENED TO THE SCREAMS, the chatter of autofire in the distance. He stopped, crouched behind a rock. Directly ahead was a cluster of trees. Through the gloom he made out the line of boulders that appeared to flank the trail.

The screams stopped, but the autofire roared on for long moments.

Then an ominous silence blanketed the slopes.

Turning his attention up the slope, Bolan saw the cabin a couple of hundred feet above at the top of the trail. Through a break in the trees by the trail, he made out the shapes of heads bobbing over the rocks. Men scurrying to climb the trail, to make their way to the cabin, Bolan knew. The distance, the poor light in the woods, obscured any positive identification by the Executioner of those men.

Bolan radioed Grimaldi for a long overdue check-in. "Jack, come in."

"Right here, Striker. Am I glad you finally called in!"

"It doesn't sound good from your end, Jack. What's the situation?"

"Grim, big guy. It seems there's some sort of installation out here. Must be a secret government-funded institute, a research facility. Looked like a hospital to me, but my guess is it's an asylum."

"I've already run into a few of the outpatients, Jack. They're either hopelessly criminally insane, or they've been drugged. My guess is both. They attack without warning, without reason. Like a bunch of damned zombies."

"Hell, they're killing machines, Striker, every last one of them. That place was a slaughterhouse. I checked the whole building. Everyone there, guards, staff, were shot to death or hacked up. Somebody set those people loose."

"KGB, Jack. It smells. I spotted a pack of those lunatics headed for town. I want you to get Kelly and Baknov out. I'll be there on the double. Out."

Silencing radio contact, Bolan pushed ahead, angling up the slope.

If the zombielike mass of killers made it to Taskinoma before Grimaldi did, Bolan knew his friend would find another slaughterhouse. And Grimaldi could find himself caught in a web of murder and insanity.

Bolan had to finish this war.

In case another war started.

And if that war had already started, then there was a good chance he could lose the Soviet defector.

FREEMAN AND THE TEN SURVIVING Long Knives topped the trail. Gasping for breath, the Long Knives gathered near the doorway of the cabin.

"I swear, Snake," Weeb Jordan threatened, "if we get out of this..."

"What do you mean, 'if,' man?" This was his chance, Freeman decided, to recover some of the face he'd lost. They were out of the reach of the CIA paramilitary force. Freeman could regain some control over his troops, he knew, if he came up with a solution to get them out of the mess they'd blundered into.

"Listen, the prize catch is right inside the cabin here," the leader of the Long Knives said. "If those spooks want the traitors so damned bad, they're gonna have to give us our weapons back, and let us outta here.''

"Snake," Jordan retorted, "you're forgettin' the CIA dudes still have the guns."

Freeman looked around the plateau. The tree cover ended at the cabin. To his immediate left, Freeman stared out across the broad, snowy valley. It was a sheer drop beyond the ledge, four hundred feet down.

"Okay, we'll grab the traitors," Freeman said. "We'll take cover in those woods. There has to be some kind of weapon inside. A knife, an ax, anything. We threaten to kill the defectors unless the spooks give us our guns and let us go." He reached for the latch on the cabin door.

The Long Knives rushed into the cabin, bumping into each other to get out of the cold. Once inside, they all stared dumbfounded for a long moment at the brutally punished faces of the two Americans.

One of them opened his eyes. He tried to say something but the gag muffled his voice.

"What the hell..." Jordan muttered, noticing the crates piled along the wall.

Freeman ignored the crates, crossed the room. Reaching the Americans, the Long Knife leader noticed the bloody stumps where fingers had once been on the hands of the two traitors. Their KGB torturers, Freeman saw, had done something to cauterize those stumps, tied tourniquets around their arms to stem the flow of blood.

The Long Knives gathered around Freeman.

"Son of a..." Jordan breathed. "They cut their fingers off."

Freeman removed the gag from across Dover's mouth.

"G-get out," the former agent warned, his head lolling, his eyes rolling back in his head as he fought to stay conscious. "The c-crates...explosives...set to..."

Freeman and Jordan looked at the crates, then noticed the wires running to the bases from beneath a plank at the doorway. The two leaders of the Long Knives looked at each other, naked fear on their faces. Behind them, Long Knives bolted toward the doorway.

Weebie Jordan muttered a curse.

It was the last thing he ever said.

A VOLCANIC ERUPTION of rolling fireballs blasted the cabin into nothingness.

Bolan froze, looking up as debris and slabs of rock rode the fiery crests of a half-dozen consecutive HE bombs. The detonation shook the ground beneath Bolan's feet. Firelight blazed across the sky. Thunder rolled on and on over the valley.

Moments later, rubbish rained down the slope around Bolan.

Wood shards.

Hunks of stone.

And bloody bits of human flesh splattered the virgin snow.

Autofire suddenly blistered the air in the distance.

It came from the other side of the trail, Bolan figured.

The Executioner charged ahead, Big Thunder ready to blast into the unknown.

FOR A SECOND, Kelly thought he was dreaming. Then he thought that perhaps he was waking from a nightmare. It was the liquor, he told himself as he pried his eyelids open. He had consumed enough booze, filled his lungs with so much cigarette smoke that his brain was clouded even to the awareness of his own nightmare.

But then, as he noted the horror on the face of Baknov, he realized those screams were real. And so was the sound of automatic weapons fire.

Kelly jumped up off the bed, accidentally kicking the bottle of Cutty Sark to the floor.

Baknov leaped from his chair and moved to the window like a man who'd just been jolted by an electrical charge.

An adrenaline surge helped clear Kelly's head, and the SOD man beat the Soviet defector to the window. Standing side by side, both men stared down at the snow-covered street of Taskinoma. At least ten bodies littered that street.

Kelly watched, rooted to the spot by fear and confusion. Below him, a mob of kill-crazed psychos attacked townsmen who rushed from the doorways of their stores and homes. Autofire drilled several townsmen through plate-glass windows. In a mindless frenzy the pack of lunatics ran down those Taskinomans who attempted to flee the slaughter.

Kelly was witnessing a bloodbath of mind-boggling, nightmarish proportion.

People were dying everywhere. But why, he asked himself. And who the hell were those psychos?

The SOD man heard the autofire that ripped through the saloon below him. He snapped his head in the direction of the door, listening to the shrieks of the dying, the banshee screams of their attackers. The sound of glass shattering throughout the town reached a crescendo, as Kelly saw the weapon-wielding tide of crazies break down doors, blast open windows with AK-47s.

Kelly knew he couldn't stay put.

He had to get himself and Baknov out of Taskinoma. And there would be no avoiding an encounter with the crazies.

It became horrifyingly obvious to the SOD man that the psychos meant to kill anything and everything that moved.

"Come on, comrade," the specialist said, tight-lipped, moving across the room. "Looks like this is our cue to get the hell out of Dodge."

THE KGB FIRETEAMS had them hemmed in, Blake knew.

There was no cover. There was no way out. There was no alternative but for them to fight until every last man was dead.

They were outnumbered.

They had been suckered into the trap by the KGB.

Blake saw Captain Benedict go down, ComBloc tumblers stitching the chest and face of his second in command. The killshots hurled Benedict back down the slope.

Bark stung Blake's face. The roar of scissoring autofire became a deafening death knell.

He managed to squeeze off a killing round, saw a Russian face vanish from his sight behind the boulder up the slope. Then a searing fire tore through Blake. He crumpled to the snow, his legs bloody, useless meat. Another slug drilled into his shoulder from behind.

He glimpsed his men, shadowy figures darting from tree to tree.

But there was nowhere to run.

The Soviets began lobbing frag grenades.

Blake saw two more of his soldiers shredded into bloody rag dolls as the blasts ripped through his forces.

It wasn't over.

It couldn't end like this, he heard his mind scream.

He thought about the failed hostage rescue mission in Iran.

He thought about Vietnam.

He had failed.

They would all go down in history as failures.

Then, a 7.62 mm ComBloc round punched through the back of Blake's head.

KOVEKNY ORDERED HIS TEAM to advance. He fell behind his troops, as they moved up the slope.

He had watched the Americans activate the time-delay mechanisms on the triton blocks as they entered the cabin, had seen and heard the subsequent mighty explosion.

He knew the KGB had defeated the CIA.

The fools.

They had come there to retrieve two American pieces of garbage. They had come there to fight to the death. And for nothing.

But the deaths of the Americans were not in vain, he knew. Their defeat at the hands of the KGB would clearly show who was the superior fighting force in the intelligence world.

And the damage that tne two American agent-defectors had mounted against the capitalist defense system had already been done years ago. The American traitors had served their purpose well.

Even in death.

But where was the great traitor, Baknov? Kovekny wondered.

Kovekny had to find out. He wasn't sure at the moment how he would get the answer, but he knew that he must discover the final reality of this deception before returning to Moscow.

In glory.

Kovekny saw the last of the CIA operatives go down. The two KGB fireteams converged on the kill-zone. They moved in tight, checking the bodies of the Americans.

A heavy silence stretched down the wooded slopes.

Kovekny started to move out from his tree cover.

From twenty yards above the KGB position, Bolan lobbed the frag grenade. The explosive landed right in the heart of the Russian murder squad. The Executioner followed that throw with another hurtling bomb.

Before most of the Soviets realized what was happening, the first grenade blew. More than half of the twenty-one men survived the blast. Within seconds they would wish they hadn't.

The second explosion took out four goons as their numbers scattered. Panic descended over the Soviets.

The mini-Uzi blazed in Bolan's left fist. A long, raking burst of SMG fire found quick targets.

Then Big Thunder roared, split the woods with mighty peals.

Two Soviets who searched for the source of the hellfire with their blistering AKMs were kicked off their feet with .44 slugs.

With deadly precision, Bolan dropped three more Russians as they fled down the slope, seeking deeper cover.

Bolan ejected the mini-Uzi's spent clip, slapped a fresh magazine into Little Lightning.

Slowly, combat senses still on full alert, the Executioner stepped away from the ring of boulders.

As he checked the killzone, a KGB gunner leaped up from the carnage, swinging his AKM toward the tall, whitesuited shadow.

Bolan was prepared for just such a ploy.

Whirling, Bolan stitched Stevhkin across the chest with a 3-round Uzi stutter.

The Executioner gave the hellzone a quick but thorough check. He waited a moment to see if there were any other Soviet takers.

There were none.

Swiftly, the Executioner moved down the slope.

He needed Baknov, alive and in one piece.

War-honed instinct told Bolan to hasten his strides.

Next stop: Taskinoma.

19

Kelly wasn't about to cat-and-mouse it out of Taski-noma. He needed a piece of ComBloc hardware. And he needed it in one hell of a hurry.

He wanted to save his own skin, for damn sure, but he wanted to keep the Soviet defector alive, too.

And he wasn't about to hang around and wait for Bolan's return or the triumphant entry into besieged Taskinoma by the CIA paramilitary force. That was assuming, of course, that his own people even walked away from the zone. Hell, it was getting late in the day and Kelly was beginning to wonder just what the score on the battlefield was.

"Let's keep moving, comrade," he told Baknov as they headed down the hallway toward the stairs. "I don't think the cavalry's gonna arrive in time. Just keep your eyes open, and stick close."

Kelly listened to the shattering of glass, the scuffling of heavy footsteps from below in the saloon. The chatter of autofire had momentarily ceased down there.

But the room was full of crazies. Kelly would bet on it.

As he began moving down the stairs, a figure swung into his view. The man held a huge meat cleaver above his head. Kelly saw the blood dripping off the blade.

The attacker screamed, tromping up the steps.

Baknov froze behind Kelly.

But the man from the Special Operations Division advanced. There was no such thing as defensive fighting, he knew. Always attack. Move forward.

The SOD man met his adversary halfway down the stairs. With a front snap kick, Kelly splintered the guy's jaw. The explosive blow also broke his neck. The meat cleaver banged off the steps, followed the man's tumbling dead-weight down the stairs.

At the bottom of the steps, Kelly peered around the corner. The saloon had been hit by a cyclone.

A lunatic cyclone.

Taskinomans littered the floor. Pools of blood spread away from the strewed corpses.

Five knife- and ax-wielding psychos were now trashing the saloon. Axes cleaved off chunks of the mahogany bar. Flailing arms swept rows of bottles off shelves. Mirrors shattered into dozens of cascading glass shards as the lunatics hurled debris into their wild-eyed reflections.

Kelly spotted a discarded AK-47. But the assault rifle was at the far end of the room. He decided he would have to fight his way through the inmates. He didn't have time for a lot of hand-to-hand bullshit, but the cards had been dealt. He wondered how badly his reflexes had been impaired by Cutty Sark, but he decided there was only one way to find out.

"Sit tight, comrade," Kelly told the Soviet defector, and stepped out into the open. Walking toward the crazies he told himself, Heart. All in the heart.

He steeled his mind.

The adrenaline rush seemed to clear the liquor fog out of his head.

Pick the vital area of the target. Deliver blow.

Glass crunching beneath his feet, the SOD man stepped right into the hellzone.

The first lunatic charged Kelly, ax raised high above his head. A bloodcurdling war whoop burst from the psycho's lips. It became his death gurgle. Kelly snapped out with a side kick. With trip-hammer force, the SOD man pistoned his foot deep into that lunatic's solar plexus. As the psycho doubled over, slumped to his knees, Kelly cupped the guy's jaw with one hand, braced the top of his head with the other. A vicious twist broke the man's neck.

Kelly sensed the movement around him, allowed his body to draw the psychos' mindless rage into him like a magnet. There was no hesitation on the part of the lunatics. They seemed possessed, driven only by a primal need to kill.

Reflected on the dangling shard of glass behind the bar, Kelly saw a lunatic rush him from behind. He reacted with lightning speed to the frenzied attack, sidestepping the rampaging attacker.

The butcher knife thudded into the bartop beside him, Kelly drove his knuckles through the lunatic's sphenoid bone.

Kelly saw steel flashing toward his face. He grabbed the knife-wielding wrist and clamped his other hand over that lunatic's sac, squeezed, lifted the psycho over his head. The SOD man sent that shrieking psycho on a missile ride, face first into the hanging piece of glass on the other side of the bar. Turning with catlike speed, he saw his fifth and final attacker rushing him, waving a meat cleaver.

Timing.

Kelly held his ground. When the lunatic was right on top of him, the specialist dropped to one knee. Throwing his weight into the psycho's lower legs, Kelly flipped the mindless killer over his shoulder. He heard the crunch of bone as face met bar.

It wasn't enough.

The madman leaped to his feet, bellowing in rage, his face a slick red mask, contorted by a feral snarl.

Kelly jumped to his feet, launched himself into a reverse sweeping kick. The side of the SOD man's foot slammed into the lunatic's face, splintering jawbone and teeth. The lunatic slid down the bar, appeared dazed for a moment. Incredibly, he held on to the meat cleaver, staggering to his feet.

The psycho surged toward Kelly, sweeping the meat cleaver back and forth.

Kelly backed away. Retreat, too, could be turned against the attacker.

The SOD man stopped. As the blade swept past him, he lunged forward, clamped a viselike grip over the wrist of the weapon hand. Kelly drove a kick into the back of the madman's knee, then followed up with a knife-edged hand to the lunatic's throat, crushing his windpipe.

Kelly walked toward the AK-47.

He turned to Baknov. "C'mon, comrade," he called out.

No reply.

Kelly looked back at the stairs. He muttered a curse as he bolted across the room, jumping over the bodies of dead men and women. Frantic, the SOD stopped at the foot of the stairs, looked up the stairs.

"Damn!"

A banging sound.

Kelly swung his head right, saw the back door swinging shut.

With a bound Kelly reached the door, opened it. From the doorway he searched the area behind the buildings. Then he looked north. Nothing there but hills cloaked by mist. He cursed. Why would Baknov just take off like that? Fear? Desertion in the final hour? What?

Kelly stepped out onto open ground.

And found Baknov.

A band of lunatics was dragging the Soviet defector away from town. They were clubbing him with blunt instruments. One of the psychos carried something like sticks in his hands. But they had a good hundred yard head start on him, and Kelly couldn't tell what it was that the lunatic carried.

The specialist started to run after the pack of crazies.

Suddenly, something jumped out of a doorway. Kelly only saw a blur, a shadow with a blazing AKM. Triggering his AK-47, Kelly drove that gunman back into the building with a hail of 7.62 mm flesh shredders.

A lunatic swept through the doorway of the saloon behind Kelly, opened up on the SOD man with his assault rifle. The madman's first three rounds tore into the backs of Kelly's legs. Kelly felt fire in his legs as they turned to jelly on him. Another slug drilled through his lower back.

The SOD man toppled to the snow, bullets dancing across the smooth white surface around his face. He rolled onto his side, the Kalashmikov still bucking in his fists. Agony and panic seemed to mesh the insides of his whole body into one flaming ball. He kept his finger on the trigger. His return fire ravaged the doorway, blasted off strips of wood, finally sheared away cloth and flesh as ComBloc lead found lethal marks. The lunatic twitched in the doorway, slammed off the frame, plunged to the snow.

Kelly gritted his teeth, saw the snow soaking up his life's juices. He'd been hit bad. Fatally, he knew. He cursed his misfortune.

There was a ragged hole in his stomach from the exit of the slug. A wound canal the size of a small fist. Blood flowed freely from the hole.

He turned over on his stomach. At the goddamn least, he thought bitterly, he could die in a warm place.

On his elbows, he began crawling back toward the saloon. He only hoped there was an unbroken bottle of the best liquor in the house left.

It was the least fate could grant him in his dying moments.

GRIMALDI SET the helicopter down on the eastern fringes of Taskinoma.

For a moment he stared ahead, his mind trying to comprehend the insanity he was witnessing. The street was a hellzone.

Minds gone mad.

Grimaldi grabbed his M-16 and four spare clips. He thrust open the cockpit door and jumped out. Instantly bullets peppered the cockpit bubble, spurted puffs of snow in front of Grimaldi. He picked out the two psychos firing on him from the boardwalk. Grimaldi triggered two 3-round bursts, drove the pair of madmen into each other with the death charges.

He had to find Kelly and Baknov somehow in this abyss of murder and frenzy.

There was only one way, he knew.

And that was to fight his way straight through the heart of hell.

He prayed that the big guy would arrive soon.

Grimaldi mowed down the lunatics with sweeping M-16 bursts. Expending the first clip, he rammed home a fresh mag. Taskinomans were fleeing the crazies, running out of town.

Grimaldi couldn't leave any of the lunatics standing. They were like automatons, programmed for slaughter. They would butcher every last man and woman in Taskinoma unless he did something to stop them.

A madman dragged a woman through the doorway of a hotel. She screamed as the crazy lifted his ax.

Grimaldi cut that lunatic in two with a quick burst, moved on.

Quickly, he checked the buildings. He found Taskinomans cringing in fear beneath beds or hiding in closets.

With every building check he came across crazies. He went through another 30-round magazine, throwing a blanket of death over the fevered brains of the madmen.

Grimaldi came out ot tne general store. Remembering suddenly that he'd last seen Kelly heading for the saloon, he ran across the street.

Inside the saloon he found another deathbed.

But he found the agent from the Special Operations Division

Kelly had pulled himself across the floor on his elbows. Grimaldi saw the trail of blood that the guy had left in his wake.

Quickly, the pilot moved to Kelly. The dying agent looked up. For a moment, he didn't recognize Grimaldi. Blood flecked the guy's lips. Grimaldi looked at the SOD man's blood-drenched legs, the soaked patch of crimson on Kelly's back.

"F-flyboy..."

Grimaldi bent over the SOD man. "Kelly. Where's Baknov?"

"Th-they got him. The loonies...I did my damnedest...."

"Where?"

Kelly tried to focus his glazed stare on Grimaldi. He coughed, winced. "Sit me up..."

Grimaldi knew the agent didn't have much time left. He'd lost a lot of blood, and as he sat Kelly up against the bar, he saw the gut shot.

"Th-they took him away...headed to the hills... west.... He was alive last I saw...."

"How long ago?"

"I don't know...thirty minutes..."

It would only be a matter of moments, Grimaldi knew, before the SOD man drew his last breath. Grimaldi had to go after Baknov, but if the lunatics had left town on foot, he figured he could catch up to them within moments by chopper. And he figured he at least owed Kelly his moment's dignity in death. They were, after all, soldiers on the same side. He was about to ask Kelly if there was something he could get for him.

Then the SOD man made his last request.

"Find me a bottle . . . whiskey if they got any. . . ."

Kelly coughed, waited as Grimaldi searched the ruins behind the bar.

Moments later, Grimaldi came back, handed Kelly a bottle.

"It's all I could find."

Kelly raised the bottle to his lips with a trembling hand. He took a long swallow, liquor sloshing down the sides of his mouth.

"Th-thanks, you're okay. . . ."

Grimaldi looked at Kelly, watched as the man took another slug of vodka.

"Our guys?"

"I have a feeling the other side's been taken care of, Kelly."

"Y-yeah, sure . . . your buddy, the Executioner . . ."

Kelly started to raise the bottle to his lips. He looked at Grimaldi, froze. He tried desperately to say something.

Then the bottle fell from Kelly's hands. A death sigh rattled past his lips.

Grimaldi brushed Kelly's eyelids shut. He stood, gave the carnage one final sweeping glance.

The KGB had turned those madmen loose, he was certain now.

The KGB.

One death machine had freed another death machine.

Grimaldi looked down at Kelly. A good soldier, yeah. There was no question in the pilot's mind about the guy's bravery or determination to combat man's evil.

Grimaldi left that hellhouse.

As he stepped out onto the boardwalk, ready to cut down the first lunatic who came into his gun sights, he saw a black transport truck race into town.

The truck stopped when it passed the chopper.

A moment later, Grimaldi felt instant relief.

Mack Bolan stepped out of the cab.

20

They kept kicking him, pummeling him about the head and shoulders. They had to drag him because his mind had gone blank, and his muscles would not respond.

Baknov figured that if they hadn't killed him yet, then a chance to escape their clutches might present itself soon.

He hoped.

Ahead, he saw the mouth of the gorge. But he couldn't see beyond because of the swirling mist. It didn't matter. He had to break free. He wasn't sure what the madmen were going to do to him, but he feared the worst.

Suddenly, he longed to return to his homeland.

Perhaps if he gave up that master list to the head of the KGB.

Perhaps if he somehow undid the damage he'd done by alerting the CIA to KGB activities against NATO.

No, he knew, that was impossible.

He would be debriefed. Then shot.

He was a dead man.

He felt the sharp edge of the knife as it slashed through his coat.

BOLAN WAS A MILE out of Taskinoma. In the distance, he saw the Bell. Grimaldi was flying over the hills, giving him recon and possible air fire support.

Together, both men had freed Taskinoma of the murderous insanity that had besieged the town. It had consumed precious time, but the Executioner wouldn't let any more innocents die at the hands of KGB treachery. Precious, critical time, he thought, in the life of one Soviet defector, Andrey Baknov.

Now Bolan steered the Russian transport truck across the snow plain. He had to salvage something from this war.

At the moment, neither side could claim victory.

All combatants were dead.

Any hope of some decisive outcome rested with Baknov.

And the master list.

The Executioner had the feeling he was blazing head-on into a new horizon, another war with the KGB murder machine. To take that war once again to the KGB, the butchers who financed and supported international terrorism, all depended on the life of one man.

The Executioner's radio handset crackled to life with Grimaldi's voice.

"I've got seven targets in the gorge, Striker. The fog makes it hard to see them clearly. They're breaking off, it looks like. Two coming your way. The others climbing to higher ground.''

"Search the hills, Jack. I'm going in.''

Bolan bore down on the mouth of the gorge. In the distance he saw two shadows step through the mist. Autofire opened up from the mouth of the ravine.

Bolan ducked as the windshield imploded under the leaden hail. He floored the pedal as slugs drummed into the hood of the truck, punched through the cab.

Crouched low behind the wheel, Bolan sent the truck rampaging ahead. Moments later, he felt the impact of metal against flesh and bone. A body cartwheeled over the hood.

The autofire stopped.

But only for a moment.

Bolan jammed on the brakes. He glanced at the passenger's side-view mirror, saw the lunatic disappear from his sight as he moved behind the truck.

Big Thunder in hand, the Executioner flung open his door.

He came out of the truck, firing. One .44 round lifted the lunatic off his feet, kicked him down on his back. The AK-47 in the madman's hands blazed skyward as his finger held back on the trigger for a second.

Bolan heard the whine of rotors to the west, saw Grimaldi clear the fog. To the west and to the north the sky had broken open. A midnight sun burned down on the snow plain.

Bolan saw something at the far end of the gorge. The figure appeared to be a man, leaning up against the front of a tree.

Reaching inside the cab, Bolan flicked on the headlights. Light knifed through the mist, outlined the figure as a dark upright shadow.

Bolan looked up at the rimrock on both sides. Swiftly, he moved into the gorge, hugging the rock wall.

Two zombies stepped into the gorge ahead. Assault rifles clattered.

Bolan dropped those two lunatics with head shots, the thunder of the death reports rolling around in the gorge. As he moved down the gorge, he heard the sudden roar of miniguns. Bolan looked up. Grimaldi had spotted enemy numbers.

The Bell swept down along the rimrock, strafing the crest with miniguns and a quick 40 mm cannon shoot.

Chunks of rock and bloody meat rained down on the snow in front of Bolan.

Grimaldi's voice came over the radio. "I'll take them as I find them, Striker. I don't see any more, but I'll keep looking."

The Bell soared past Bolan.

Within moments, the Executioner made it to the end of the gorge.

And he found Baknov.

For the Russian defector the horror was over. Almost.

Whatever sickness, whatever insanity had burned in the minds of the psychos had manifested itself in what they'd done to Baknov.

Bolan closed down on the last hope of victory on the Alaskan slopes.

The inmates had stripped Baknov, driven steel spikes through both wrists, into the tree. They had even allowed for gravity, the pull of Baknov's weight, that would eventually tear his hands free of the spikes, by impaling him on a wooden stake.

Bolan lifted the Russian's face. "Baknov. Baknov!"

The Russian's eyelids fluttered open.

"The master list. Where is it?"

Blood ran down Baknov's bare legs. The stake had been shoved up through his intestines.

Baknov's lips slitted. "D-Damascus...Mossad... agent...Ph-pharaoh..."

Pharaoh? Bolan thought. A code name.

"Baknov? Who is Pharaoh?"

Baknov's eyes rolled back in their sockets. His head lolled off to the side.

The faint bleat of the Bell's rotors broke through Bolan's anger. Then Grimaldi's voice rasped over the radio handset in frantic tones.

"Mack, behind you!"

Bolan whirled, saw the shadow at the other end of the gorge an instant before the muzzle-flash parted the mist. Bolan nosedived to the ground, slugs ripping into the naked corpse of Baknov.

A line of deadly AKM fire tracked Bolan before he secured cover behind a boulder.

The AKM in Sergey Kovekny's hands roared on as the KGB assassin raked the gorge.

Slugs whined off the stone above Bolan's head, but he managed to make out the sound of the shouted Russian words. Bolan realized that Kovekny had hidden himself in the back of the transport truck after he suspected that Baknov was being held somewhere in Taskinoma.

The KGB goon had come along for the ride.

Unslinging the mini-Uzi, Bolan lunged up over the top of the boulder at the first lull in fire. He triggered a quick burst, but Kovekny climbed into the truck, gunned the engine to life.

Kovekny surged the rig forward, barreling down the gorge.

Bolan plucked an MK2 off his webbing, pulled the pin. He hurled the grenade, timing his throw, gauging the distance between himself and the truck.

The grenade hit the snow several yards in front of the truck. A second later, the frag blast ripped off the front of the truck, hurtling debris. The explosion flipped the truck over on its side. Gas ignited, a fireball instantly consuming the cab.

The Bell hovered in the mouth of the gorge as Bolan stepped out from behind the boulder.

"Striker, what the hell was that?"

Bolan spoke into his radio handset. "A loser, Jack. The last player just crapped out."

Slowly, Bolan walked toward the flaming wreck-age.

He sheathed Big Thunder, strapped Little Lightning around his shoulder.

The horror was over. For now, at least.

As sure as the midnight sun would set, the Executioner knew the black dice would roll on.

Tomorrow.

Somewhere else.

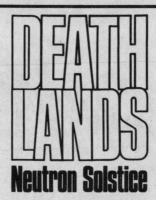

4 FREE BOOKS
1 FREE GIFT
NO RISK
NO OBLIGATION
NO KIDDING

TAKE 'EM NOW

FOLDING SUNGLASSES FROM GOLD EAGLE

Mean up your act with these tough, street-smart shades. Practical, too, because they fold 3 times into a handy, zip-up polyurethane pouch that fits neatly into your pocket. Rugged metal frame. Scratch-resistant acrylic lenses. Best of all, they can be yours for only $6.99. **MAIL ORDER TODAY.**

Send your name, address, and zip code, along with a check or money order for just $6.99 + .75¢ for postage and handling (for a total of $7.74) payable to Gold Eagle Reader Service, a division of Worldwide Library. New York and Arizona residents please add applicable sales tax.

Remove from pouch...

unfold once...

Gold Eagle Reader Service
901 Fuhrmann Blvd.
P.O. Box 1325
Buffalo, N.Y. 14240-1325

unfold twice...

and they're ready to wear.

Offer not available in Canada.